Property of
AMERICAN CANYON
MIDDLE SCHOOL

Dust from Old Bones

Dust from Old Bones

SANDRA FORRESTER

MORROW JUNIOR BOOKS
NEW YORK

Published by Morrow Junior Books
a division of William Morrow and Company, Inc.
1350 Avenue of the Americas, New York, NY 10019
www.williammorrow.com

Printed in the United States of America.

1 3 5 7 9 10 8 6 4 2

Library of Congress Cataloging-in-Publication Data
Forrester, Sandra.
Dust from old bones/Sandra Forrester.
p. cm.
Summary: The diary entries of thirteen-year-old Simone Agneau, a child of mixed African and European ancestry, reflect the peculiar caste system in Louisiana before the Civil War.
ISBN 0-688-16202-9
[1. Race relations—Fiction. 2. Racially mixed people—Fiction. 3. Afro-Americans—Fiction. 4. New Orleans (La.)—Fiction. 5. Diaries—Fiction.]
I. Title. PZ7.F7717Du 1999 [Fic]—dc21 99-19035 CIP

For
Carolyn Fine,
because you loved the story,
and because you do so much
to make everything better.
With thanks and love.

Dust from Old Bones

I speak of sins and failures
betrayals that linger
of angels that watch
and flutter
stirring
dust from old bones.
The story has been told before.
It will be told again.

Preface

The Louisiana Territory was colonized by France in 1702, relinquished to Spain in 1762, and returned to France in 1800. The United States purchased the territory from France in 1803; but as late as 1838, the year in which *Dust from Old Bones* takes place, Louisiana remained European in its tastes and customs.

Louisiana Creoles, who were descendants of the original French and Spanish settlers, valued their European heritage above all else. Most were French-speaking Catholics who viewed themselves as aristocrats—at the top of the rigid caste system they had created. White Americans, and white settlers from Canada, were on a lower stratum of Louisiana society. Black slaves from Africa and from French colonies in the Caribbean were at the bottom.

And then there were the free people of color.

Descended from the offspring of slave mothers and Creole fathers, many of these people became skilled craftsmen or prosperous merchants. Some acquired wealth as planters and slave owners. Others entered the professions of law and medicine or excelled as artists, poets, and musicians. The children of this affluent class were often educated in private schools and sent to the best universities in France. They lived in fine houses in New Orleans, spoke fluent French, and had the manners and attitudes of Creole ladies and gentlemen. But they were never accepted into Creole society, because of their mixed African and European ancestry. Thus, the free people of color, or *gens de couleur libre,* were forced to create their own society, which they patterned after that of the Creole aristocracy.

The daughters of the *gens de couleur libre* had fewer choices than the sons. They could marry another free person of color, or they could enter into an arrangement with a wealthy white man who would provide them with a house, a comfortable life, and security for the children they had together. Laws forbade interracial marriage, but these relationships were regarded as quasirespectable and often lasted for many years—in some cases, for a lifetime.

The female offspring of these unions were generally pampered from birth. They grew up believing themselves to be superior to anyone whose manners were not as refined, whose skin was darker, or whose speech was less genteel than theirs. Many of these young women felt they had little choice but to continue in the tradition of their mothers, believing that a privileged life with a wealthy Creole was preferable to marrying a shopkeeper or craftsman of mixed race.

The *gens de couleur libre* were never free. They could not vote or hold public office. They were expected to be deferential to whites at all times. They could be arrested for striking a white person, even in self-defense. The strange blend of privilege and prejudice that marked their lives must have been all the more painful for those who were educated in France, where they were free from racial discrimination. It is not surprising that many of the *gens de couleur libre* chose to remain in Europe, where they could finally emerge from the shadows.

April 1838

Thursday 12 April

MY NAME IS Simone Marguerite Racine. I am called Simone by everyone except Papa, who calls me Ti-Simone because, he says, I am his little girl. I fear that Papa's eyesight is failing—for my legs have grown as long as those of his favorite mare—but Papa is decidedly pigheaded and unlikely to change his ways.

If I seem to be preoccupied with livestock, it is only because I have never kept a personal journal and hardly know how to begin. Madame Sardou insists that keeping a diary in English will help me with my grammar—which she says is atrocious!—though I wonder why it matters, since my family and friends, and everyone else in New Orleans who matters, speak only French. When I said as much to my cousin, Claire-Marie, she replied, "But what if you should marry an Américain, *chérie*?" And we both laughed. As though a Creole woman would ever consider such a thing!

It was Claire-Marie who gave me this beautiful book, in honor of my thirteenth birthday. So I write in the hope that she will be pleased that I am putting her gift to good use—and in the greater hope that Madame Sardou will cease to sigh and grumble that I am butchering the

English language. Though how else she will spend her time, I cannot imagine.

Friday
13 April

MADAME SARDOU SIGHS and grumbles still. Before class on Monday, I must write a five-page composition in English. Of no surprise to me, Claire-Marie's recitations were perfect.

Claire-Marie is one year older than I. She is not only my cousin but also my dearest friend, even though she *is* Madame Sardou's pet. Claire-Marie is the sole child of Vivienne, Maman's younger sister. Unlike me, Claire-Marie is beautiful. She is small and her features are delicate—very French—as are Maman's and Tante Vivienne's. Her skin is creamy white and her hair falls as straight and shiny as raw silk down her back. I have heard it whispered all my life that Claire-Marie could pass for white. My skin is only slightly darker than my cousin's, but I could not pass. I study Claire-Marie often without her knowing, and I see that should she choose to *passer à blanc*, she could. But that would mean leaving New Orleans, where everyone knows who and what we are, and Tante Vivienne would never agree to that, for she has grand plans for Claire-Marie.

Maman has called me to help Azura with dinner.

From the scent of peppers and onion and orange in the air, I presume we are having gumbo and *beignets d'oranges*. I do love Azura's gumbo, but I sorely detest stirring the soup pot. The heat causes my hair to frizz, and cayenne pepper makes me sneeze. When I suggest to Maman that cooking is Azura's job, not mine, *ma mère* says I am insolent and lazy. But why have a slave at all, I ask, if *I* must do the onerous chores while *she* stands idle?

Tante Vivienne does not make Claire-Marie help with dinner. They have two slaves to cook and serve and clean, while we have only one (not counting me). Life is unfair.

Later

WHEN PAPA AND my brothers arrived at midday for dinner, I was setting the pot of gumbo on the table. Papa sniffed and said, "*Merveilleux*, Ti-Simone! What an accomplished wife you will be." But Maman declared that my husband and children will be little more than rattling bones if they wait for me to find the kitchen. I have a blister on my hand from the soup pot, and Maman's sharp tongue to contend with, as well. Life is *decidedly* unfair.

Perhaps I should take a moment to write about my

family. My father is Jean-Louis Racine and he is the kindest, dearest papa in the world—though less indulgent with my brothers. Papa is an artist. He carves beautiful monuments and statues from stone. My mother is Delphine Agneau Racine, the eldest of Jules Agneau's three daughters. Grand-père Jules is old and his health is failing. Maman takes him baskets of fruit each day and flowers to brighten his rooms. When she gives him strawberries, Grand-père shouts that he wanted blueberries, but Maman is a dutiful daughter and does not take offense. She is also a dutiful wife and mother, but she expects gratitude from her husband and children. More often than not, I disappoint her—in this regard and others.

Sadly, I have no sisters—except for Claire-Marie, who is as dear to me as any sister—but I have two brothers. Gabriel is eighteen and learning the art of stone carving and sculpture. Papa says he is gifted. My favorite brother, Celestin, whom we call Tin-Tin, is fifteen and has just begun to work with Papa. Tin-Tin is anxious to have a chisel and mallet in his hands, but for now, he is only allowed a broom to sweep the studio floor.

When I was small and Papa spoke of Gabi and Tin-Tin working with him someday, I thought I, too, would be a sculptor when I grew up. But Papa told me that stone carving is not proper for a woman. The work is too hard and dirty, he says, so I settle for sketching in charcoal and pastels. But I love the feel of marble beneath my hands and long to create something beautiful from a block of fine stone.

When Papa and the boys returned to the studio in rue Bourbon, I asked to go with them. I wished to see the monument Papa is carving for Monsieur Belmain's little son Emile, who died from cholera. Papa has devoted months to sculpting a white marble angel in the likeness of the boy, and soon it will be delivered to the section of St. Louis Cemetery where the *gens de couleur* are buried. But Maman would not permit me to go. She said there was silver to polish and linens to press. She will not allow me to set foot in Papa's studio for fear I might soil my dress and slippers—while the boys may *wallow* in stone dust, for all she cares!

As I polished the silver, I thought of floating through the swamp on Lucien's raft—happy thoughts so that I would appear pleasant should Maman look in. But I did not *feel* pleasant. Why must we have forks and spoons at all? Would it not be more sensible to use our fingers and lift our bowls to sip as the negroes do?

Saturday
14 April

AT LAST, MAMAN has gone to her room to rest and I have some peace. I brought my sketchbook to the courtyard, but even though a breeze stirs the palmettos, the air is heavy and I am too lethargic to work at my drawing. So I sit beside the statue of St. Anthony de Padua and study his solemn face. St. Anthony is supposed to bring good fortune to everyone in our home. I am still waiting for him to realize that I live here.

Through the gate, I see the old negro woman Henriette pushing her cart as she sells pineapples and bananas door-to-door. Down the rue Dumaine, I hear other vendors cry, "Fresh fish! Crab! Fresh fish here!" and "Strawberries, strawberries! Get your fresh strawberries!"

Something moves at my feet. I see a flash of bright green as a tiny lizard darts across the brick to the tangle of bougainvillea vines that covers the side of the house. My eyes follow the flutter of vines as the creature ascends to the balcony above. That is when I see Azura. She moves as quickly as the lizard along the gallery, her skin as black as Papa's boots against the white of her dress and the faded pink wall. There is something secretive in her movements as she hurries down the stairs to the courtyard. So I slip behind the statue of St. Anthony and watch.

To Papa and Maman, Azura is simply a maker of good gumbo, a trusted servant who keeps the brick walks scrubbed and the house smelling of lemon. They have not watched her as I have.

She follows a path through the willows and palms to the other side of the courtyard, her apron pockets sagging with the weight of candles from Maman's cupboard. She disappears into her cottage and shuts the door. Then she draws a curtain across the window, so I cannot see what she is doing. But I know. For years, I have watched the people come to Azura at night, pleading with her in whispers, crying softly into their hands. They ask for charms and amulets, spells and magic powders. They ask Azura to light the candles: green for driving away unwanted spirits, yellow for wealth, blue for protection from curses—or to cause death! And for a price, Azura will give them what they desire. For Azura is more than the maker of good gumbo—she is also the maker of powerful *voudou.*

Sunday dawn
15 April

LAST NIGHT, AFTER Maman and Papa had retired and the house was still, I crept down the back stairs to the kitchen and filled a napkin with the jelly cake, nuts, and raisins left from supper. Then I went to the courtyard and climbed the staircase that leads to my brother's *garçonnière*. It is assumed that young Creole men have a need for their own staircase and private quarters—and my older brother has certainly made good use of them.

Gabi was out with his friends, as he is most Saturday nights. Maman does not like it when he goes to the waterfront taverns and comes home weaving from too much whiskey. But Papa tells her that Gabi is a man now and entitled to his pleasure. Maman worries that Gabi is out so late, since people of color must be inside their homes by nine. But Papa says that should the patrols see Gabi and his friends on the street after curfew, they would only send them home with a warning. After all, it is the money young men of color spend on whiskey that keeps the taverns open!

Tin-Tin's chamber was dark when I opened the door. But I heard the bed creak and then he whispered, "Simone? Is that you?"

"I brought food," I said, and closed the door behind me.

"*Eh bien,*" Tin-Tin said. "Something good, I hope."

"Come outside and judge for yourself."

"Are you here to spy on Azura again?"

"You know I cannot see the courtyard from my chamber," I replied, and stepped through his window to the roof. We sat down on the cool tiles to enjoy our midnight *pique-nique,* and to watch and wait.

It was not long before I heard the gate moan as it opened, and a woman stepped into the courtyard. A white woman—and, judging by her elegance, Creole. She crossed the open space quickly, as though she had been here before, and went straight to Azura's door. She knocked softly and the door swung open. The woman entered the cottage and the door closed—but not before I saw a circle of lit candles on the dirt floor. A thread of smoke began to rise from Azura's chimney, and a very bad smell soon reached our noses.

"It is terrible!" Tin-Tin exclaimed. "The odor makes me gag."

"Hush," I said softly. "The fire is to drive away evil spirits."

"That smell will drive away *anything,*" he muttered.

While the woman was still inside, an old negro man

in rough clothing arrived, then a negro girl wearing a striped turban over her hair. When the cottage door finally opened again, Azura emerged with the white woman, who was weeping and clutching something to her bosom. "*Merci,* Mambo Azura," the woman said through sobs. "I am indebted to you."

"Quiet!" Azura demanded, and the woman's head dropped meekly, but still she wept.

Five people had come to our courtyard and left again when Tin-Tin said, "The sun will be rising soon."

We crept back inside and I returned to my chamber. But sleep eludes me. My head is filled with imaginings of what goes on behind Azura's closed door. Lucien has seen her in the swamp catching snakes and gathering plants—dogwood root and nightshade and black sage. Lucien says the *voudou* mambos use these poisonous herbs in their magic.

Maman will wonder why my candle has burned so low and why my nightdress is covered with soot.

Sunday afternoon

MASS WAS VERY long and I dozed from time to time. Maman pinched me twice. But I suspect that even God was snoring before Père Michel completed his final prayer.

After Mass, as we strolled the place d'Armes, Maman and Tante Vivienne squeezed the fruit and vegetables, declared them too ripe or too green, and bargained for a better price. Tante Vivienne bought a blue silk shawl and an ivory fan. Papa drank coffee and discussed business with the men. Claire-Marie and I bought ginger cakes, which we ate as we walked from cart to cart and looked in shop windows. Then I saw Lucien coming across the square to sell quail and doves from the swamp.

Claire-Marie does not approve of Lucien, because his skin is dark and he wears no shoes, and because he has little schooling and works as a stable boy. She says he smells of horse droppings and swamp water. Maman agrees. But Papa—who is dark himself, and worked at many lowly jobs while learning his trade—calls Lucien "remarkable." How many boys of thirteen work six days a week, Papa says, and hunt on the seventh to support their families? I have told Claire-Marie that Lucien will not always be a stable boy, that he plans to have a stable of his own one day, but Claire-Marie says he will still smell of horse droppings.

When Lucien saw me, he waved. Claire-Marie left to promenade with the women.

"*Comment to yé*, Simone?" Lucien greeted me. It is true that he has had little education and speaks the lazy

French of negroes, which is called Gombo. Still, we understand each other well enough. He was eager to show me the plump birds he had caught, but the sight of their poor, lifeless bodies made me feel quite ill.

Lucien smiled. "You make a face, but you are quick to eat them once they are roasted, eh, *chérie*?"

About this, he is right. And that is one of the things I like about Lucien: He speaks the truth but does not judge.

Lucien asked if I would care to go to the swamp again, assuring me, as he always does, that we will be safe from alligators and wild hogs on his raft. I have no desire to see alligators' great gaping jaws within inches of my feet, or snakes dropping from limbs into the water, but I do enjoy sketching the strange flowers and moss-draped trees. I agreed to go whenever I can slip away.

The swamp is mysterious and beautiful and terrible. So silent, and yet alive with creatures that lurk in the wet darkness. To even think of it makes me shiver. Still, I have gone to the swamp with Lucien many times. On the one occasion that Maman learned of this, she lectured me for running about the city with a negro boy and for wasting time better spent doing my duty. For weeks afterward, she made certain that my duty was not neglected for a moment—if, indeed, it is my duty to embroider more pillow slips than one could use in a lifetime and to pray to Our Mother Mary until calluses form on my knees. Since the Virgin Mother cares so tenderly for outcasts and other despised creatures, I feel certain she heard me the first time. But Maman apparently fears that Our Blessed Mother is either prone to memory lapses or is as deaf as a turnip.

Monday
16 April

TODAY, AS WE walked the rue St. Anne on our way home from school, Claire-Marie said suddenly, "The old man is dying, you know."

Shocked by her words, I said, "He has been ill before, but he always recovers."

"Not this time," she replied. "The doctor told Maman that Grand-père will not last the summer."

"But *my* mother has said nothing to me."

Claire-Marie turned to look at me, and I thought I saw pity in her eyes. Then I knew it when she said, "Tante Delphine keeps her own counsel. You know she does not confide in anyone."

But I am her daughter! I wanted to cry. And I felt a rush of sorrow because Claire-Marie is right—Maman is distant with everyone, even her husband and children. I also felt angry with Claire-Marie. She can be as thoughtless as a child or an ill-bred slave. What right does she have to make careless remarks about Maman's conduct?

"Tante Delphine never changes, and that is her way," Claire-Marie continued. "Maman says it is because of what happened long ago in Haiti. Tante Delphine was the eldest, so it was harder for her."

I could see that Claire-Marie expected me to respond, but I said nothing. Maman refuses to speak of those times, and so it hardly seems proper to discuss them with my cousin!

Perhaps sensing my disapproval, Claire-Marie finally said with a shrug of indifference, "What happened when our mothers were children is of little interest to me. I care about today and tomorrow, not yesterday."

If only it were that simple, I wanted to tell her. Does she not see that what Maman and Tante Vivienne experienced those many years ago follows them to this very day?

It is time for bed, and Maman has told me to put out my candle. I will write more tomorrow.

Tuesday
17 April

I TOSSED AND turned late into the night, thinking about Grand-père Jules—is he really dying?—and

Maman, and what I know about their lives in Haiti.

Maman has never spoken to me about her childhood. Once, when I was very small, I asked her a question about when she was a little girl. I do not remember the question, nor her reply, but I will never forget how angry she became. After that, I did not question her about the past again.

It was Tante Vivienne who told Claire-Marie and me about Haiti. I was eight or nine, and spending the afternoon with my aunt and cousin, as I often did in those days. We were sitting under the pomegranate trees in their courtyard, sipping lemon tea, eating pralines, and listening to the carts rattle down the street, when Claire-Marie suddenly asked her mother, "Was Grand-père very, *very* rich when you lived in Haiti?"

I expected Tante Vivienne to laugh, as she usually did at one of Claire-Marie's indiscreet questions, but she did not even smile. In fact, my aunt was clearly disturbed by the question and it took a moment for her to reply, "*Oui*, your grandfather was very, very rich. He owned one of the largest sugar plantations in Saint-Domingue."

Since then, I have learned that there were many wealthy men of color living in Saint-Domingue before the slaves revolted against French rule. Madame Sardou has told us about the revolution, of how all the whites living in Saint-Domingue were either killed or driven from the country. Then the former slaves declared Saint-Domingue's independence from France and changed its name to Haiti. Next, they waged a war against the people of color who had been free before the revolution. Wealthy planters were forced to leave their homes and flee the country—as Grand-père Jules did when he came to New Orleans.

After she had answered Claire-Marie's question, Tante Vivienne seemed to withdraw from us, and even Claire-Marie realized that she should ask no more. Tante Vivienne did not speak again for a long while. And that is unlike my aunt.

Tante Vivienne is normally as talkative as *ma mère* is silent. They look very much alike, but that is where the similarity ends. Maman is a serious, practical person. Papa says, with pride, that she keeps a more organized home than any other woman he knows—that she can tell you at any moment how many pounds of coffee beans are in the pantry. I suspect that Tante Vivienne has no idea *what* is in *her* pantry. She leaves the running of the house to her slaves—Azura's daughters, Paulette and Eulalie—so that her days are free for shopping and dress fittings. If I were to ask her how many pounds of coffee beans she has in the house, my aunt would laugh and say, "How should I know, *chérie*? And why should I care?" Indeed, I have wondered this myself.

The silence continued, and then, quite suddenly, Tante Vivienne said, "I was eight years old when the war began." She was staring into the jungle of yucca, bamboo, and camellias that grew with abandon in the courtyard, and she seemed to be speaking to herself. "There were six of us children, three girls and three boys."

Claire-Marie's head jerked up. "You had brothers, Maman?"

"They were babies," Tante Vivienne said. "Auguste was two and the twin boys had just been born. Our mother was staying with her *maman* until she regained her strength. The twins were with her, of course, as was Auguste. My sisters and I remained at home with Papa."

"How old were Tante Delphine and Tante Madelon?" Claire-Marie asked.

"Delphine was ten and Madelon was only four."

I had heard about Tante Madelon. Of course! Who does not know of the wild and strong-willed Madelon Agneau? But I have no personal memory of her. She left for Paris when I was small, and she never returned. Once, Claire-Marie told me that Tante Madelon had married a white man, a French artist named Nicolas Girard. But that is all I know. Since she ran away to Paris, Grand-père forbids anyone to speak her name.

Tante Vivienne told us they were preparing for bed

the night the men came. Many negroes with torches and guns.

As she spoke, my aunt—who is always so gay, whose eyes are always filled with laughter—appeared grave, and there was nothing but pain in her eyes.

She told us that the former slaves came to the plantation house and our grandfather's slaves joined them against Grand-père. They shattered the glass in the windows and set fire to the house. They broke down the door and rushed inside even while the house was in flames. Then they destroyed the furniture and tossed it like sticks of kindling into the blaze. She told us that she and Madelon hid under the bed, and Madelon screamed. Delphine found them there and dragged them from their hiding place.

"If we stay here, we will die," the ten-year-old Delphine, my mother, told them. Then she carried Madelon and pulled a terrified Vivienne down the back stairs.

The house was filled with smoke and the shouts of men who ran to escape the inferno. Madelon still screamed, and Vivienne—who held so tightly to Delphine's hand that, later, she realized her nails had ripped into Delphine's palm and left it dripping blood—called over and over for her papa.

Somehow, Delphine found her way through the

smoke to a back door and got her sisters outside to safety. Vivienne was coughing and blinded by the smoke, but she felt strong arms embrace her. “Papa!” she cried. But when he whispered words of comfort to her, she realized that it was Bodin, her father’s negro manservant.

Tante Vivienne said Bodin took her and Maman and Tante Madelon to the fields, where he hid them among the cane stalks. She said that he found their papa, shot and left for dead, and carried him to the cane fields, as well. And it was Bodin who moved them to an abandoned slave hut and brought them food and nursed their papa until he began to heal.

I have known Bodin all my life. He opens the door to Grand-père’s house, looking fine in his linen shirt and crisp black coat. He never smiles or even speaks except to say, “I will tell Monsieur Jules you are here.”

“But Grand-père should have freed him,” I said. “He saved your lives.”

“Bodin did not want his freedom,” Tante Vivienne said. “He wished to stay with Papa.”

She told us that Grand-père Jules was still very weak when he rode to his father-in-law’s plantation to see about his wife and sons. But nothing was left of the plantation house except smoldering ash. His wife and his sons, and his wife’s mother and father, were all dead. Tante Vivienne remembered Grand-père returning to the slave hut. She says, even all these years later, she could still see the blood-chilling hatred in his eyes that day.

"They have tried to destroy me," he said to his daughters. "But they have failed. *They will not destroy me!*" he shouted to the sky.

The little girls were frightened by their father's rage, and Madelon began to cry. Grand-père grabbed Madelon's shoulders and shook her.

"Stop that!" he demanded. "Tears are weak!"

My mother pulled Madelon from him and embraced her. "Papa, she is only a baby," Delphine said.

"She is an *Agneau*!" Grand-père thundered. Then he looked at them with eyes so cold and hard that Vivienne began to tremble. Delphine pulled Madelon and Vivienne close, as though trying to protect them from their father's fury. But still he stared at them with those cold eyes, and he said, "You are *all* Agneaus. *Never forget that.* They took my sons, but I still have daughters. It will have to be through you that the Agneau name lives on."

The child Vivienne could not stop trembling. But my aunt still remembered the feel of Delphine's arms around her, strong and reassuring.

"Papa's fortune was in his land," Tante Vivienne told us. "We arrived in New Orleans with enough money to buy the house in rue d'Orléans but little else.

It was left to Delphine, Madelon, and me to regain what Papa had lost. The money, the power, the family name...." Tante Vivienne seemed to have left us again as she murmured, "It was left to us to restore the House of Agneau."

I did not understand what she meant then, nor do I now. Sometimes I repeat her words to myself and try to divine their meaning. *It was left to us to restore the House of Agneau.*

Thursday
19 April

I HAVE BEEN watching Maman more closely of late. How efficiently she goes about her work: sorting clothing to give to Père Michel for the poor, planning menus with Azura, inspecting the table linens for stains and wear. Never is she idle. Never does she complain. And when our neighbor's servant comes to say that madame is ill, Maman goes at once with rice tea and tonic. Everyone says of Maman that she is a good woman, a practical woman, a strong woman. She is all these things, and more. But I fear she is not a happy woman.

When I was younger, I would sometimes sleep at Claire-Marie's house. Tante Vivienne would help us into our nightdresses and tuck us into Claire-Marie's bed under the rose silk canopy. And then Tante Vivienne would climb into the bed herself and tell stories that made us laugh, or sing songs about nightingales and angels. And always she would hold us and kiss our faces and call us "*ma petite*" and "*chérie.*" I would wonder why Maman never kissed me or told me stories. I longed for her to! But as Claire-Marie says, that is Maman's way.

Friday
20 April

MADEMOISELLE ESMÉ IS making Claire-Marie dresses, and Maman says I am to have new ones, as well! A blue muslin for everyday wear and a white Chinese crepe for Sundays. Maman disapproves of Tante Vivienne's extravagances—especially the huge sums she spends on Claire-Marie's wardrobe, not to mention her own. And yet, when Maman hears that Tante Vivienne has ordered kid slippers for Claire-Marie, she orders identical slippers for me. Papa cannot afford so many gowns and slippers as Claire-Marie has, and Maman says that no young girl should be spoiled so. But even while she criticizes Tante Vivienne's spending, I suspect that Maman envies her.

Of course, Tante Vivienne has nothing of her own. It is Edouard Larousse, Claire-Marie's father, who bought the house in which Tante Vivienne and Claire-Marie live. And it is he who pays for their wardrobes and Claire-Marie's tuition and the French wine Paulette serves with their meals. Monsieur Larousse owns a sugar plantation thirty miles downriver. That is where he lives with his wife and the children who bear his name. Claire-Marie has never seen the plantation, but she says it is very large and that her papa is rich. Monsieur Larousse rarely comes to New Orleans, so Claire-Marie sees him only three or four times a year, but she adores him. I am not permitted to visit when he is there, but I have seen him arrive in his grand carriage. He is younger than Papa, and handsome. His hair is as pale and fine as the silk on new corn.

Monday
23 April

SCHOOL WAS MOST pleasant today. When I had completed my recitation in English, Madame Sardou said, "Your grammar is not so horrendous as it once was, Mademoiselle Simone." Which is infinitely better than shaking her head from side to side and crying, "No, no, no! You will be the *death* of me!"

Claire-Marie was also pleased. She gave me a kiss and an orange. Could this journal possibly be working?

Madame Sardou read to us about a Frenchwoman named Jeanne d'Arc who lived a long time ago. When she was a little older than I am, Jeanne heard the voices of angels telling her to save Charles, the dauphin of France, from the approaching English army. She rallied the French troops and led them into battle, fighting alongside them even after an arrow pierced her shoulder. In another battle, she continued to fight with an arrow in her thigh. The English finally withdrew and Charles was crowned king of France. But Jeanne was later captured by the English and then tried in France as a witch. Charles did nothing to save her, and she was burned at the stake.

Madame Sardou says Jeanne d'Arc should be revered for her piety and selflessness, but I am inclined to believe she was rather stupid. I asked Madame Sardou where Charles was while Jeanne was risking her life for him.

She was annoyed by my question. "He was inside his castle," she replied impatiently, and turned away before I could ask more.

Inside his castle, *indeed*!

Wednesday 25 April

AT SCHOOL TODAY, Claire-Marie could speak of nothing but the six dresses Mademoiselle Esmé is sewing for her. The girls were envious—even Julia Bernadin, whose father buys her dresses when he travels to New York. But those are *American* dresses, and Mademoiselle Esmé orders her fabric and patterns from Paris. Minette, who is my second-best friend, told them that Mademoiselle Esmé is also making two dresses for me. The girls murmured, "How nice," before they turned back to Claire-Marie to hang on to her every word. I should not mind, but at times I wish I could have something that Claire-Marie does not have. Just *once*!

Thursday 26 April

MAMAN FINALLY TOLD me that Grand-père's health is failing. She said I must visit him very soon.

"Of course," I replied, hoping she would not see the dread I feel. What a spoiled, selfish girl I am! But *mon Dieu*, what a difficult man he is!

I told Tin-Tin that he must go with me.

"I am busy with my work," he said. "Besides, caring for sick people is a woman's duty."

Much annoyed, I replied, "Your broom will be waiting when you return."

My brother laughed, not the least offended, and left the house whistling.

Tin-Tin is no longer my favorite brother.

Monday 30 April

WHEN I WENT home with Claire-Marie to see the patterns for her dresses, I was shocked to learn that three of them are evening gowns for a grown woman!

"But where will you wear them?" I asked, imagining what Madame Sardou would say if Claire-Marie came to school with her shoulders bared.

"To the balls, of course," Claire-Marie said gaily.

I must have looked puzzled, because she laughed. "The *balls*, Simone—the quadroon balls."

"But you are only fourteen," I protested. "Surely that is too young for the quadroon balls."

"I am old enough," Claire-Marie said firmly. "Arabelle Thiers and Honorée Cuvier were fourteen when they went to the balls." She smiled, her eyes soft and dreamy. "I have planned it all. One gown will be pink satin with black lace trim and silk roses at the waist. One will be cream silk embroidered in white, with a white lace shawl. And one will be dark blue satin with pearls across the bodice. I will wear my hair swept up with flowers that match my gown."

"Tante Vivienne approves of this?" I asked.

Claire-Marie looked surprised. "But of course. You know what Maman wants for me—a protector as wonderful as my papa. Fine Creole gentlemen will come to the balls," she added, her face flushed with excitement. "And one of them will see me and ask me to dance. And then he will speak to Maman. And she will tell him that I must have a house and a generous allowance, and that our sons must be educated in France. Oh, Simone, I know he will be handsome and rich and romantic. I can hardly wait to meet him!"

I want to be happy for Claire-Marie. I have always known that this is what Tante Vivienne had planned for her, but I thought Claire-Marie would be older. Sixteen, perhaps. Maman says that is how old I must be before I marry. I thought we would have more time before everything changed.

"Why the frown, my little cousin?" Claire-Marie asked gently. "I know your mother wishes you to marry a man of color, and that will be right for you. But I want something else, *chérie.* I have never met him," she added softly, "but I see him in my dreams. He will be tall like my papa and his hair will be the color of wild honey. Our children will have white skin and golden curls. And our sons will be wealthy, accomplished men. Maman says that Grand-père's dream for our family will be realized through my sons."

We had tea with Tante Vivienne, but I cannot say what we ate or what was said. I was so miserable at the thought of losing my cousin to this unknown Creole, I could think of nothing else. Tante Vivienne and Claire-Marie seemed not to notice, but Paulette handed me a covered plate as I was leaving for home. "Perhaps you will feel like eating later, mam'selle," she said.

For the first time, I looked closely at Paulette. She is not much older than Claire-Marie, and her sister, Eulalie, is even younger than I. They have Azura's black satin skin and large dark eyes. But there is nothing secretive in Paulette's and Eulalie's eyes, and their smiles are sweet and trusting. They do not seem to mind that they are slaves, and I wonder why this is. *I* would mind terribly! Even now, I dislike how others direct my life and do not ask what I desire. And how, one day, Papa and Maman will introduce me to the man who will be my husband. He will own a prosperous business and his skin will be light brown. He will be gentle, for Papa would not allow me to marry someone who is unkind. And our children will be strong and beautiful. But they will not have white skin and golden curls.

May 1838

Thursday 3 May

TANTE MADELON IS coming home! Grand-père received word from her yesterday.

"Maman read the letter," Claire-Marie said as we walked to school. "She says it was filled with expressions of love and remorse. Tante Madelon begged Grand-père to forgive her for staying away so long. She said she did not know of his illness until Tante Delphine's letter arrived."

"Maman wrote to her?"

Claire-Marie went on as though she had not heard me. "Maman says Madelon is only coming home so that Grand-père will include her in his will," Claire-Marie declared. "Maman is supposed to inherit the house, and when she dies, it will be mine. But Madelon will expect him to leave it all to her."

I held my tongue, but I wanted to say, What about *my* mother? She is the oldest. Should Grand-père not leave her something?

Claire-Marie was so preoccupied, she did not even smile when the boy who sells flowers on the corner handed her a rose and bowed as though she were the queen of France.

"Maman says that Madelon was willful and conniving even as a child, but Grand-père did not see that—he was blinded by her charming ways," Claire-Marie continued. "She was his favorite, but when she left, he turned to Maman. My mother stayed while Madelon was marrying her artist and living a frivolous life in Paris."

Again, I resisted the urge to speak. Tante Vivienne sees Grand-père once a week, perhaps, and leaves soon after she arrives. Sick people make her melancholy, she says. I cannot blame her for being unable to tolerate the old man—even when he is in good health!—but Maman visits Grand-père every day and sits with him for hours. If his illness makes her melancholy, she does not mention it.

"I will not like Tante Madelon, Simone," Claire-Marie said fiercely. Then she seemed to notice the pink flower in her hand for the first time. With an impatient shake of her head, Claire-Marie flung the rose to the street.

Saturday
5 May

WHAT A TERRIBLE day! I went with Maman to visit Grand-père Jules. She carried a basket filled with oysters, mushrooms, and a bottle of brandy. I took a loaf of freshly baked bread. It was not my fault that I dropped the bread and a cart filled with chickens ran over it. I retrieved most of the loaf and brushed it clean of dirt, but Maman was not satisfied. She tossed the bread into the gutter, yanked me by the arm, and ripped the lace on my sleeve. This, she also blamed on me!

Grand-père lives in the rue d'Orléans, near St. Louis Cathedral. The house is large and beautiful, but it seems as forbidding as death to me.

Fig and orange trees grow in the courtyard. Shimmering red-colored fish swim in the fountain, which has a kneeling lamb carved at its base. The door knocker is also a lamb, in honor of Grand-père's name—Agneau—which means "lamb." That is how the house came to be called Lamb House by everyone, or, more correctly in French, House of the Lamb.

Maman lifted the lamb's head and knocked. Bodin opened the door instantly. I have often wondered if he stands there all day, just waiting for someone to knock.

"How is he today?" Maman asked.

"The same," Bodin answered, and took the basket of food from her. "Your sister Vivienne is with him."

In fact, Tante Vivienne was coming down the stairs.

"He is losing strength," she said. "It is good you

came, Simone." Then to Maman she added, "Why ever did you write to Madelon, Delphine? Did you know she will be here in a few days?"

"Should she not see her father before he dies?" Maman responded.

"Well, *you* have nothing to lose by her coming," Tante Vivienne snapped. Then she sighed. "But it is too late to stop her now. I suppose we must welcome our sister with open arms."

Grand-père was lying in his great bed with the four mattresses. His eyes were closed. The draperies were drawn and his chamber was filled with shadows. Perhaps that is why I did not see the cat at first. I might not have noticed it at all, nestled as it was in the rumpled bedding, had Grand-père not shifted restlessly and disturbed the animal's sleep. The cat stretched and cast an indifferent amber glance at Maman and me before resettling its large gray body across Grand-père's legs. That my grandfather would permit this creature in his house, much less his bed, came as a shock to me.

Véronique was mixing medicines on the bedside table. She held up a glass filled with dark liquid.

"Time for your tonic, monsieur," she said.

Grand-père's eyes opened and he snorted. "More *voudou* potions to prolong my dying? Take it away!"

Maman walked to the bed and bent over him.

"Papa, do as Véronique tells you," she said firmly.

The old man glared at Maman. His features are French, but his skin is brown and he has the thick, coarse hair of an African.

Véronique held the glass to his lips and he gulped the liquid down. Then he fell back against the pillows. "Now, leave me be!" he ordered.

Véronique is as light-skinned as Maman. She carries herself with grace and dignity, even though she is a slave. "I will be back in two hours," she said.

"No more potions!" Grand-père shouted to her retreating back.

"Two hours," she repeated over her shoulder, and left the room.

"I should have her flogged," he muttered. Then he looked at Maman. "What did you bring me?"

"Oysters—"

"You know I prefer shrimp!"

"And mushrooms and brandy—"

"Are the mushrooms fresh?" Grand-père demanded. "The last you brought were too stale to eat."

"They are fresh, Papa," Maman said patiently. Then her eyes shifted to the sleeping cat and she stared hard at the creature. "Since when do you have animals in the house?" she asked. "Cats carry every sort of vermin, and this one looks none too clean."

"What I keep in my house is no one's concern but mine," Grand-père shot back. "And I happen to prefer the company of dumb animals to that of humans."

Then he seemed to notice me for the first time. "So your daughter found a moment to visit an old man, Delphine." He frowned as he studied me. "What is your name again, girl?"

"Simone, monsieur," I said politely, but I know he could see the indignation in my face. I have been going to his house for thirteen years; of course he remembered my name!

"Delphine, you permit your daughter to come visiting in a torn dress?" he asked sharply.

Maman's eyes slid to my sleeve, then to my face. She looked angry—not with him, but with *me*!

"She has little beauty," Grand-père continued, his eyes boring into my face, "not like Claire-Marie. But that hardly matters in her case. You must be industrious and obedient, as your mother is," he said to me. "That is what a shopkeeper looks for in a wife."

I left the room as quickly as I could slip away. Maman was reading to him, and they did not see me go.

Véronique was in the courtyard picking basil from her kitchen garden.

"You did not visit long," she said.

"I stayed as long as I could bear it." I sat on the edge

of the fountain and rested my feet on the back of the lamb. "Since when has he taken a liking to cats?"

"Since that one followed me home from the market and moved in," Véronique retorted. "It crept up the stairs to your grandfather's chamber. Bodin was going to put it out, but monsieur would not hear of it. So it lies in his bed growing fat from quail and cheese from monsieur's own plate!"

"I cannot say much for the animal's choice of companions," I said.

A smile flickered across Véronique's lips. "He is a trying man, your grandfather."

"*Mon Dieu!*" I exclaimed. "He is the devil!"

Véronique laughed. "*Oui,* sometimes he is that. What did he do to upset you?"

"He said that I must be industrious and obedient," I said bitterly. "That my plain appearance will not matter to my shopkeeper husband. But Claire-Marie's appearance will matter. My cousin will go to the quadroon balls, and she must be beautiful to catch the eye of a rich Creole!"

Véronique said nothing, but I could feel her sympathy. This only increased my anger.

"Maman is beautiful," I said. "*She* could have attracted a Creole gentleman had she wished."

"*Non,*" Véronique said softly, "she could not have."

"Why do you say that?" I demanded.

"Because Monsieur Jules would not permit it. He chose Vivienne and Madelon to go to the balls and find Creoles to father their children."

"And what of Maman?" I asked. "What was Grand-père's plan for her?"

"You should ask your mother that."

"You have told me this much," I said impatiently. "What was his plan for Maman?"

After some hesitation, Véronique finally said, "Your mother was to marry a man who could support her family until Vivienne's and Madelon's sons restored the family's fortunes. Delphine did not wish to marry a man of color—she had her heart set on going to the balls with her sisters—but Monsieur Jules approached Jean-Louis and the arrangements were made."

"No. You are lying!" But even as I spoke, I knew that she was telling the truth. I have always known that Maman wanted something her family could not provide. I sensed her frustration and her envy of Tante Vivienne, even while she disapproved of her sister's frivolous conduct. What Véronique said explains so much that I have wondered about. The life Maman has—with Papa, Gabi, Tin-Tin, and me—is not the life she would have chosen; it was thrust upon her. And how she must resent us for it.

"Your papa is a good man," Véronique said. "Has he not given you all loving care? Your mother could have done worse."

"My mother does what she is told to do," I said sharply, "as does Tante Vivienne." I wanted to lash out at Véronique. And I wanted to run to her and weep in her arms.

"You judge so harshly," Véronique said. "Perhaps when you are older, you will see things differently."

"I will see nothing differently," I said. "Grand-père is a terrible man, and Maman and Tante Vivienne are his marionettes. Tante Madelon is the only one with courage enough to defy him."

"Does it take more courage to walk away or to stay and confront the demons that beset you?" Véronique asked softly.

I was too agitated to think about her question, or to wait for Maman. "Please tell my mother that I have gone home," I said curtly, and started for the gate.

"She will not be pleased," Véronique called after me.

I did not bother to answer. My mother's displeasure mattered little to me at that moment.

Sunday
6 May

AZURA ATTENDED MASS this morning with Paulette and Eulalie, as she always does. To see her there appearing so pious was troubling. How can she do the devil's work at night and pray to God and His saints on Sunday morning?

Maman is angry because I left Grand-père and went home without waiting for her. But I am angry, as well! Why did she not defend me to him? Why did she not defend *herself* long ago? I am also angry with Tante Vivienne and with Claire-Marie. And I am even angry with Papa, who has done nothing really to deserve it. But his docile acceptance of Maman's bullying and his genuine sorrow over Grand-père's failing health infuriate me. Why must he always be so tolerant? There is such a thing as being *too* good, unless you are a saint!

And that is not all. After Mass, Claire-Marie would not walk with me. She stayed with Tante Vivienne, looking quite grown-up in her white silk bonnet with the ostrich feathers at the crown. Her behavior was perplexing. Since when does Claire-Marie care if the crabs are fresh or the lemons too green? I wondered.

And why was she whispering and giggling with Tante Vivienne as though they were girlfriends sharing a secret? Then I saw *him*. Henri Jourdan. He was watching Claire-Marie and smiling. I have heard Claire-Marie mention him casually—"His father is one of the wealthiest Creoles in the city" and "He is quite handsome, is he not?" But Claire-Marie comments on every presentable man she sees, so how was I to know she had a special interest in Monsieur Jourdan?

Today, he and Tante Vivienne carried on a lively conversation, but it was Claire-Marie he watched out of the corner of his eye. And Claire-Marie dimpled and simpered in the most disgusting manner.

I do not think him handsome at all.

Sunday evening

AFTER DINNER, MAMAN gave me pages to read in my missal. "Read and contemplate," she said.

I went to my chamber and tossed the missal under the bed.

It was excitement I needed, not contemplation! But since there was little hope of that, I thought to do a sketch of the courtyard for art class. Except the colored chalks seemed to have a will of their own, and I found myself creating a portrait of my family like none I had ever imagined.

I drew each person in a different color: Papa in wispy strokes of pale gray, so that he appears as ephemeral as smoke or fog; Maman in dark charcoal with strong, bold lines, her features seeming to have been chiseled from stone; Tante Vivienne in lavender, the strokes of color soft and airy; and Claire-Marie in yellow, bright and lovely, but indistinct.

This portrait is not the "nice" drawing I usually do—the scenes of our courtyard with St. Anthony and palmettos that appeal to Madame Sardou's desire for propriety and beauty. There is nothing beautiful about this drawing. But I am exhilarated by what I see and intend to show it to Madame Sardou. I fear she will be shaking her head and crying once more, "You will be the death of me."

But now I must write about my adventure this afternoon! After putting my sketchbook away, I climbed out the window and up the sloping roof to the courtyard side of the house. I thought that Azura would have already left for Congo Square, but I was not too late. She was just emerging from her cottage with Paulette and Eulalie. They had changed from their plain dresses to brightly colored skirts and blouses. Azura wore a red-and-yellow-striped turban and the girls had madras kerchiefs over their hair.

Watching them leave the courtyard, I decided to follow them to Congo Square and see for myself what the slaves' Sunday revelry is all about. It seems ridiculous that I have waited thirteen years to do so, even with Maman's stern warnings to stay away.

During the week, Congo Square is simply a pleasant grassy common planted with shrubbery and sycamore trees, and it is called Circus Square. But on Sunday afternoons, the slaves gather there to dance and sing and play their music—and it becomes Congo Square.

I lost Azura and her daughters in the crowded streets. It seemed that every negro in the city was headed for Congo Square. When I arrived, there were already hundreds of people gathered—men, women, and children with dark faces. So it is as Maman said: Only the slaves go to Congo Square, not our people.

Very soon, the music began. I stood under cover of the trees so as not to draw attention to myself, but I was close enough to see all that was happening.

Men with handmade instruments comprised a strange orchestra. An old negro sat astride a huge drum that he beat with his fingertips and the sides of his hands. Others had small skin drums that they held between their knees. Some musicians played crude stringed instruments and beat blocks of wood with sticks.

The music was loud and unlike anything I have heard before. It might be thought of as little more than earsplitting noise except for the enticing rhythm that drew the dancers to the center of the common. They formed circles across the grassy square and began to move in time to the music. Some had bits of metal and bone tied to their ankles with ribbon. The men stamped and dipped and leapt into the air. The women swayed from side to side and sang words I did not understand. And then, suddenly, the men would cry out, "*Danesz Bamboula! Badoum! Badoum!*"

I have heard Maman and Tante Vivienne speak in hushed tones about the savagery of the slaves' dances, and how they should be outlawed. But I think they are wonderful! Even though I could not understand what the words and movements meant, I could feel the dancers' passion. I regret not taking my sketchbook, but I will try to capture the scene from memory.

Time passed so quickly. When I noticed the sun sinking behind the trees, I knew that I had stayed too long. I ran all the way home, expecting Maman to be angry that I was not in my chamber. But when I entered the house, I found Papa and Maman napping.

The cannon has sounded to tell the slaves to disband. I hear Maman's voice, so I will close for now. I must crawl under the bed and retrieve my missal.

Monday
7 May

MADAME SARDOU STUDIED my family portrait for a long time. She looked puzzled, but all she said was, "This is very...*interesting*, Mademoiselle Simone."

I was gravely disappointed.

Tuesday
8 May

CLAIRE-MARIE SPEAKS OF nothing but going to the balls. She has not mentioned Henri Jourdan, but I imagine it is his face she now sees in her dreams. He is tall and his hair is the color of wild honey.

Thursday
10 May

TODAY I DREW another family portrait. I gave Claire-Marie a wart on the end of her nose.

Later

I REMOVED THE wart.

Monday 14 May

THERE HAS BEEN nothing worth writing until today. Now there is much to record.

Of greatest interest is this: Tante Madelon has come home and I have met her. Véronique sent word yesterday that Tante Madelon's ship had docked and Bodin was going to the wharf to escort her to Grand-père's house.

"She will be tired," Maman said. "We will wait until tomorrow to see her."

This morning, Maman sent Azura to the market for crawfish to make crawfish étouffée. And Maman made a pineapple cake, while Azura baked yams and roasted a turkey. When I arrived home from school, Maman brought out my white embroidered dress and said, "Wear this. And your new kid slippers."

Papa and my brothers were at the studio, so Maman and I went alone to Grand-père's house, with Azura carrying the food. I had vowed never to cross that threshold again, but today my curiosity was stronger than my sense of honor. I was dying to meet

Tante Madelon—and, what's more, to meet her before Claire-Marie did.

When Bodin opened the door, I saw a woman standing behind him in the foyer. She wore a gown the color of ripe apricots. A dark green stone hung on a gold chain around her neck. Her black hair was pulled back into a chignon and adorned with green velvet ribbon. Like Claire-Marie, she could pass for white. I have never seen a more beautiful woman in my life.

She moved toward Maman, a delighted smile on her face. "Delphine" was all she said. Then her arms closed around my mother and Maman returned the embrace.

When Tante Madelon finally pulled away, there were tears in her eyes. "Oh, Delphine, forgive me. I have been so selfish, *chérie.*"

I saw in amazement that Maman was dabbing at her own eyes with a handkerchief. "You are here now," she said. "In time to make peace with Papa. That is what matters."

Then Tante Madelon turned to me. Her expression was friendly and open and curious. I could not help but return her dazzling smile.

"Simone, what a lovely young woman you have become," she said. Then she was holding me and kissing me on both cheeks.

We sat in the drawing room, which has been closed

since Grand-père's confinement to his bed. It is the most elegant room in the house, with the crystal chandelier and gilt mirrors and mahogany tables from France. A fine setting for my elegant aunt.

Maman questioned Tante Madelon about her life. Tante Madelon's eyes filled with tears again when she spoke of her husband's recent death. Then she described their house and their friends, who all seem to be important poets and artists, and the gay life they lived in Paris.

"Now that your husband is gone, you must remain in New Orleans," Maman said.

Tante Madelon shook her head. "I have missed you all terribly, but Paris is my home. Nicolas and I were so happy there, Delphine. You cannot imagine the difference. In Paris, one is judged by accomplishment, wit—many things!—but never by one's race."

I also learned that Tante Madelon is an artist. Her paintings are displayed in galleries throughout Europe. She is going to turn an upstairs chamber in Grand-père's house into a studio so that she may continue her work while she is here.

I asked if I could see her paintings, and she gave me that beautiful smile once more. "When I complete a painting, you shall be the very first to see it, *chérie*," she said. "You are interested in art?"

"*Oui,*" I replied, feeling suddenly shy. "I enjoy sketching."

"Schoolgirl drawings," Maman said dismissively, and began to speak to Tante Madelon about Grand-père's condition.

But Tante Madelon continued to glance at me and smile. And before she and Maman went upstairs to see Grand-père, she said, "I would love to see your drawings, Simone. When I come to visit, will you show them to me?"

Which, of course, I will gladly do.

Tuesday
15 May

CLAIRE-MARIE AND HER mother went to see Tante Madelon last evening. My cousin agrees that Madelon is very beautiful and elegant.

"Tante Madelon will return to Paris when Grand-père dies," I told Claire-Marie. "She has no need for his house."

"So she says," Claire-Marie replied. "But we do not even know this woman, Simone. Maman says that Grand-père is already beginning to forgive her. When they were together, Tante Madelon teased him in the most outrageous manner and he was not even sharp with her."

I do not care what Claire-Marie and Tante Vivienne say. *I* think Tante Madelon is extraordinary!

Wednesday 16 May

MADELON SAYS I have talent! I thought, perhaps, she would forget about my drawings. But when she came to visit this afternoon, she asked if she could see them.

"Bring your sketchbook down here," Maman told me. But Madelon said, "I would enjoy seeing your chamber, Simone. May I come with you?"

Maman looked surprised, but, of course, she would not be ungracious to a guest. I was glad Madelon came upstairs with me, for I wished to show her my family portraits and could not have done so with Maman there.

Madelon studied each of my drawings carefully. She was silent for such a long time, I grew increasingly anxious. But then she looked at me and said, "These are wonderful. The courtyard scenes are lovely, but it is the portraits that interest me most. They are so alive! You must continue to draw, Simone. To use your feelings as you have with these portraits. I know you can become an accomplished artist."

Then she asked if I would like to learn to paint in oils. I would like nothing better! She spoke to Maman, who hesitated and then said that I might. "But I do not want Simone taking all of your time," Maman added.

Madelon smiled at me, apparently as pleased as I was. "I have so little to fill my days while Papa sleeps," she said. "I will be grateful for Simone's company."

I am to have lessons three times a week!

Thursday 17 May

IT SEEMS THAT everyone is angry except for me. And Tin-Tin, of course, who is content with his life and wants nothing more.

At supper, I was telling Papa about my painting lessons with Madelon. He was agreeable, as I knew he would be, for Papa loves to see me happy. I was telling him that Madelon learned to paint from some of the finest artists in Paris when Gabi said, quite suddenly, "I would like to go to Paris and study sculpture." I have always suspected that Gabi longed to go to France, as some of his former schoolmates have done, but he has never mentioned it to Papa. Nor should he have, apparently, because it made Papa very angry. He told Gabi that they are *craftsmen*, not artists, and that Gabi would do well to put those silly ideas out of his head.

"But you said I am becoming a fine stone carver," Gabi protested.

"*Oui,* but you are not a Creole dilettante," Papa snapped. "You must earn a living, as I do. We haven't the luxury of spending our days in Paris cafés and calling ourselves artists."

Gabi stormed from the house. Three hours have passed and he has not returned.

But that was not the end of it. After Gabi left, Maman—who was quite distraught—said to Papa, "Why must you always be so harsh with him?"

"Because he is not a child," Papa replied. "It is past time he gave up these foolish ideas of being a Creole gentleman."

"I have raised both my sons to be gentlemen," Maman said in a cold voice.

"And filled their heads with impossible dreams," Papa responded. "Next, you will be having Simone follow Claire-Marie to the quadroon balls."

Maman looked shocked, then angry. "Simone will marry a *craftsman,*" she said sharply. "There will be no Creole *gentleman* for her."

Papa threw down his napkin and left the house as Gabi had done. Papa has not returned, either.

I have never seen Maman and Papa behave so. But

the harder I try to understand what happened, the more questions I have. I know that Papa is disappointed because the bank will not give him a loan to expand the studio. He told Maman that the city is quite happy to collect high taxes from him, but its leaders do not wish men of color to become too prosperous. Perhaps that is what Papa was trying to tell Gabi—that an ambitious man of color will not be tolerated in New Orleans.

But my heart breaks for Gabi, who *is* an artist. It must hurt him deeply to have his talents disparaged by his own father, whatever the reason.

And why did Papa have to introduce my name? I seem destined to be at the center of any trouble that plagues this family.

Friday
18 May

WHEN TANTE VIVIENNE heard that I was to have painting lessons, she asked that Claire-Marie be included. My cousin has never been interested in art, but now she wishes to learn to paint. Blessed Mother, I will surely be punished for my unkind thoughts.

It appears that Maman and Papa have made up. Not that either would ever apologize, but after supper I came upon them in the courtyard. Maman was reading her favorite French poetry aloud and Papa was listening with his eyes closed. He was smiling.

Monday 21 May

CLAIRE-MARIE AND I had our first painting lesson today. Madelon has removed all the furniture from an upstairs chamber and filled it with easels and canvases. The canvas on which she is working stands in a corner and is draped so that we cannot see it until the painting is finished.

Madelon said that before we learn to paint, we must draw and draw and draw. She set up a still life of fruit and bottles, and we spent two hours sketching them. Claire-Marie's drawings were not very good. In fact, they were terrible, and she was the first to admit this. She laughed so readily at her pathetic efforts that soon Madelon and I were laughing with her.

"I have a confession to make," Claire-Marie said to Madelon when the lesson was over. "I'm not interested in learning to paint—I only wished to hear about your life. And I thought I might secretly copy the design of your gowns."

This sent Madelon and me into spasms of laughter

once more, with Claire-Marie joining in. The three of us held on to one another and laughed until we were breathless.

Madelon has decided that Claire-Marie will continue to come for lessons. But while I am instructed in painting, Claire-Marie will be allowed to sketch Madelon's gowns as best she can.

On the way home, Claire-Marie reluctantly admitted that she likes our young aunt.

Wednesday
23 May

HOW MUCH I enjoy the painting lessons! And Claire-Marie does add to the fun. Today, however, Madelon became serious when Claire-Marie mentioned going to the balls.

"*C'est dommage!*" our aunt exclaimed. "The balls are an abomination. You deserve more, Claire-Marie."

My cousin was clearly surprised by this response. "But only the finest gentlemen attend," she protested. "And girls from the best families."

"To be sold like prime livestock," Madelon replied.

"*Non!* It is not like that at all!"

Madelon said patiently, "I know all about the balls,

Claire-Marie. I was sent to them by my papa. And there *were* fine gentlemen, as you say, eager to become my protector. But they were not willing to share my home or give our children a name."

"But what does that matter?" Claire-Marie demanded. "I do not have Papa's name, but he could not love me more. When he comes to see us, the first thing he says is, 'Where is Claire-Marie, *mon petit chou*?' He asks me, 'Are you happy, *chérie*? Are you well? Do you need new dresses?' My papa loves me very much!"

"I am sure he does," Madelon said kindly. "But what if something should happen to him? The law does not allow him to leave you or your mother anything in his will."

"The house is in Maman's name," Claire-Marie said quickly. "It was part of the agreement."

"And the money for your dresses and lessons and pretty playthings? Would that continue if your papa should die?"

"I do not wish to speak of Papa dying," Claire-Marie said crossly.

"I only want you to see that you have choices," Madelon said. Then she looked at me. "You both do. In Paris, you would be accepted into white society. You could even marry a white man, if you wished, as I did. You would have his name and inherit his property."

"I know nothing of Paris," Claire-Marie said stiffly. "New Orleans is my home."

New Orleans is my home also, and I would miss it should I leave. But when our aunt speaks of Paris, I long to go there and see it with my own eyes.

When we were leaving today, Grand-père's cat followed us to the courtyard. He leapt to the edge of the fountain and proceeded to bathe his long gray fur. I stroked his back and felt the gentle vibration of a purr.

"Stop that, Simone!" Claire-Marie said sharply. "It probably has mites and fleas and heaven only knows what else. Will you never grow up?"

"What does petting a cat have to do with growing up?" I demanded. But Claire-Marie just shook her head and continued toward the gate.

"*Au revoir,*" I called defiantly to the cat, and his amber eyes followed me to the street.

Thursday
24 May

WE STOPPED AT the market for coffee and cakes on the way to school, and Henri Jourdan was there. Claire-Marie lowered her eyes and smiled prettily, and he looked like a man bewitched. I pushed Claire-Marie through the crowd, saying we would be late, but

I know he watched her until we were out of sight.

Perhaps he is a *trifle* handsome.

Friday
25 May

I SKETCHED THE Congo Square dancers and musicians from memory and showed my drawing to Madame Sardou. She looked stunned, and then she cried, "Put these away, mademoiselle! Or better still, toss them into the fire. *Mon Dieu, mon Dieu,* whatever will you think of next?"

Her response was gratifying.

Later

MADELON'S REACTION TO my sketch was very different. "*C'est beau,* Simone! How wonderful! You have captured the movement, the excitement, the feelings!" Then she decided that we would walk through the city so that I could sketch from life. Claire-Marie did not wish to walk and so went home.

At the waterfront, I sketched while Madelon drank coffee and talked to the people and bought a basketful of trinkets. I asked why she was not drawing and she laughed, her cheeks flushed as she took in the activity around her. "And miss all the excitement?" she demanded. "Conversing with people is so much more entertaining than sketching them."

But I found people on the docks fascinating subjects for my drawings—the beggar woman crouched on the wharf with her hand stretched out to passersby; a negro woman in a silk *tignon* with a basket of shrimp balanced on her head; and Madelon's favorite—a drunken sailor who sprawled on the levee singing naughty songs and waving whiskey bottles in the air.

"Do not show this one to your mother," my aunt said, her eyes filled with mischief.

How different she is from Maman!

Sunday
27 May

MADELON ATTENDED MASS with us. Then we strolled the place d'Armes. Later, during dinner at Tante Vivienne's, Madelon said, "The white men in this city gaze at women of color as though they wish to devour them. They would never leer at white women that way."

"My days of attracting a stranger's attentions are past," Maman said placidly.

"I suppose it is not like that in Paris," Tante Vivienne said sharply.

"*Non,*" Madelon replied. "It is not like that at all."

Paulette and Eulalie served so many dishes—Tante Vivienne trying to impress Madelon, no doubt. Madelon smiled and thanked them each time they brought her food. This seemed to annoy Tante Vivienne even more.

When we were walking home, I offered to accompany Madelon to Grand-père's house. After we had left the others, I said, "I have never seen anyone thank servants for waiting on them—Maman says it is their duty."

"Is there a reason why we cannot be kind to them?" Madelon asked.

"Of course not," I said hastily. "Papa and Maman are never unkind to Azura. But Maman says the negroes are happy in their place, and if we are too friendly with them, they will feel uncomfortable."

"Do you agree with that, Simone?"

I did not know how to answer because I had never considered it before.

"Well, *I* believe Paulette and Eulalie are no different from you and me," Madelon said briskly. "They were just unlucky enough to have been born into slavery."

Never in my life have I thought of Paulette and Eulalie as being like me! Again, I was silent.

"Your great-grandmother was a slave," Madelon

said. "Did you know that? No, I can see that you didn't. She was light enough to pass for white, but she was still a slave. So we are not that far removed from slavery ourselves, are we?"

"But Paulette and Eulalie are African," I said. "I am part white."

"And part negro, as well," Madelon replied. "Did you know that Azura came from Saint-Domingue as we did? Before the slave rebellion, she was brought to New Orleans by the Frenchman who owned her. Azura could be related to us."

This was too much for me to entertain! "But Azura is a *voudou* mambo. We could not be related to a devil worshiper."

"Oh, Simone," Madelon said softly. "Azura's spells and gris-gris are harmless. She practices *voudou* because people pay her well for it. And perhaps because it gives her a sense of power. Imagine what it must feel like to be owned by someone and have no control over your life."

I did not need to imagine, since I have so little control over my own life. But I did feel a prickling of sympathy for Azura and her daughters.

"So much in life is luck," Madelon said. "Whether we are born rich or poor, slave or free. You and I have more luck than some," she added. "And less than others."

Monday 28 May

WHEN MAMAN LEFT to visit Grand-père, I went to meet Lucien. I took a pair of Tin-Tin's old boots—the ones he wears when he and Papa and Gabi go hunting—and put them on as soon as Lucien and I approached the swamp.

Lucien keeps his raft tied up in a small inlet outside the city. Claire-Marie thinks he is not a gentleman, but he had brought old sacks for me to sit on so that I would not soil my dress or get splinters.

The raft is nothing more than a dozen rough logs roped together, but it glides as smoothly as a swan through the dark green water. As we floated deeper and deeper into the swamp, Lucien showed me the places where he finds the fattest doves and geese and quail. After spending so much time here, Lucien has acquired the eyes of a swamp creature—he pointed out deer and herons that I would not have noticed in the dim quivering light.

Lucien's mother has just given birth to her tenth child. Lucien seems happy to have another brother, but I could only think that here was another mouth to feed. And since his papa was injured, Lucien is the only one bringing food into the house. I remember when Lucien's father was the strongest man on the docks. He could work all day loading and unloading ships and still have energy left to take Lucien and me fishing. But all that changed in an instant, in the time it took for a rope to snap and a crate to come hurtling down on him. Now his right sleeve hangs empty and his legs tremble when he tries to stand without a crutch. He often smells of whiskey. Lucien says his father drinks not for pleasure but to dull the pain.

Lucien lives in two cramped rooms in an alley near the wharf. They have a rough table and benches for taking their meals and thin pallets on the floor for sleeping. Lucien says that drunken men from the waterfront fight and shout obscenities all night outside their door. As Tante Madelon said, she and I have more luck than some.

Instead of drawing the trees and flowers today, I sketched Lucien standing at the front of the raft, guiding it with his pole. He was so pleased with the result, I gave him the drawing to keep.

It was beginning to drizzle when we left the swamp. By the time I reached home, rain poured from the sky in a torrent. I held Tin-Tin's muddy boots out the window to clean them before placing them by the kitchen door, where he had left them. I should have thought to dry them first, for later, when Maman saw the pool of water on the kitchen floor, she declared that the roof was leaking. Tin-Tin is up there now, searching for missing tiles. He asked to come down until the storm ends, but Maman only shook her head and shouted, "Keep looking!"

I will say twenty Hail Marys for penance—or forty, perhaps, since I cannot help laughing when I picture my brother crawling across the roof like a half-drowned river rat. And I will tell Tin-Tin that mending the roof is a *man's* duty.

Tuesday
29 May

CLAIRE-MARIE HAS BEGUN to wear her hair in a chignon as Madelon does. The resemblance between the two is striking. When I am with them, I could easily feel gauche—and sometimes do—but Madelon praises my small hands and smooth complexion.

Wednesday
30 May

TODAY ON OUR walk through the city, Madelon expressed a desire to see inside the new St. Louis Hotel. I was amazed by its grandeur. Never have I seen so many chandeliers and mirrors, such rich draperies and beautifully attired people.

Madelon said this is where the wealthy come to dine and dance, and where Creole planters stay when they come to New Orleans during the opera season. This is also where they come to buy and sell slaves.

Along with the grand ballrooms and dining salons, the St. Louis houses the slave exchange. I have never been permitted to go near the slave block, but today Madelon and I happened upon it without knowing. It is openly visible inside the hotel!

Such a mass of negroes were crowded into the large room: tall, sturdy field hands; women holding babies in their arms; the old, the young, and some who appeared very ill. And among all those dark faces, I was shocked to see a few of mixed race, with skin as light as my own!

I cannot begin to describe my feelings when we came upon this dreadful sight. Some of the negroes were so poorly dressed, they were nearly naked, while others wore dresses as costly as those of Claire-Marie. Some smiled at the men who had come to buy, while others hung their heads in misery and sorrow.

"Blessed Mother," Madelon whispered.

I wanted to turn and leave, but my feet seemed fastened to the floor. I could not tear my eyes away from those faces!

I watched as two men led a young girl up the steps to be viewed by the buyers. A third man called out to the crowd to look at her. "Raised with her master's children," the man shouted as she was turned around slowly. "A hard worker!" he exclaimed. "Speaks passable French and can lift sixty pounds."

"Simone."

I heard my name, but I could not look away from the girl on the block. Her eyes were fixed above the heads of the men who gawked at her—beautiful black eyes that swam with tears.

"Simone, we must leave." It was Madelon who spoke, and she who guided me through the grand hotel to the street.

My legs were weak and my heart pounded. I felt so dizzy, I feared I would fall to the ground. But Madelon held on to me and the dizziness receded.

"I am so sorry," Madelon said. Her face was pale. "I knew they held slave auctions at the St. Louis, but I never would have brought you here had I known they conduct them in the open."

"The girl was crying," I said softly.

"Simone, you cannot tell your mother what you saw!" Madelon said.

"Of course not," I replied, surprised by the urgency in her voice. As though she *feared* Maman.

I will tell no one what we saw. But that girl's tear-filled eyes will stay with me forever.

Thursday
31 May

I DREAMED ABOUT the slave auction last night. But it was I who stood on the block. Madelon and Claire-Marie were in the crowd of buyers. They were speaking to each other and laughing. Then I saw Henri Jourdan. He was watching Claire-Marie with obvious interest. When my cousin noticed him, she dropped her eyes and smiled. I cried out to my aunt and my cousin, but they did not hear me. No matter how loudly I cried, they never looked my way.

June 1838

Friday
1 June

WHEN I ARRIVED at Grand-père's house for my lesson, Madelon embraced me and asked if I had recovered from our shocking experience.

"*Oui*, I am fully recovered," I told her, which is mostly true. But I still see the slave girl's face when I close my eyes.

Madelon thought it best that we stay inside today, and I was glad. I sketched the baskets and grapes and melons she had arranged for me. While I drew, Madelon sewed a lace collar onto one of her gowns.

"You could paint while I draw," I said. Her draped canvas still waited in the corner.

"*Non*, I can only paint when I am alone."

"When will *I* begin to paint?" I asked.

"Soon," Madelon promised. "You are beginning to draw with more confidence. Before long you will be ready for oils."

After a while, I grew bored with drawing the same baskets and fruit over and over. So I said, "Tell me about the quadroon balls. Were they terrible?"

Madelon looked up from her sewing. "On the contrary, Simone, they were exciting." She smiled, remembering. "The young men were most attentive and complimentary. And the music and dancing—it was all wonderful."

"But you told Claire-Marie—"

"I told Claire-Marie that she deserves more," Madelon said, finishing my sentence. "And she does. It is so easy to be caught up in the magic of the balls, but they are fantasy. Life is not ball gowns and dancing in a handsome man's arms, Simone. Real life is difficult. We must accept that if we are to survive."

"Is that why you ran away?" I asked. "To survive?"

A strange smile came to Madelon's lips. It was not a happy one. "That is exactly right, *chérie.* If I had remained in this house, I would have been living someone else's life—*Papa's* life, not my own. If I had stayed, Madelon Agneau would have died. In that sense, I did leave this house in order to survive."

"You must dislike coming back here," I said. Then, hastily, I added, "I did not mean that you dislike Grand-père—"

"Oh, but I do," Madelon said, and I could hear the bitterness in her voice. "A part of me dislikes him very much. And another part..." She shrugged. "Another part loves him because he is my papa. But enough of this serious conversation! We will leave our work and go to the market. I will buy us cakes and chocolate, and your mother will scold you for spoiling your supper."

Maman did not scold me, but she did question me about what Madelon and I do on our walks through the city.

I told her that I sketch and Madelon talks with the people we meet. "We are perfectly safe," I assured Maman, because I sensed that she was troubled by something.

"No doubt," Maman replied, but she did not seem reassured. Then she said, "Your aunt has lived a different life from yours. I hope she remembers that you are young and inexperienced."

At first, I thought she must be referring to the slave auction. Somehow she must have found out that Madelon and I were there. But if that were the case, she would not have hesitated to make her displeasure known! So I am left wondering what it is that Maman fears. And knowing her, it may never become clear.

Tuesday
5 June

I WAS AT Claire-Marie's house when her father arrived. His carriage had barely pulled to a stop when Claire-Marie ran outside to fling herself into his arms.

Tante Vivienne called for Paulette to clear away our dishes, then ran to the mirror to pinch her cheeks and smooth her hair.

"Simone, you must leave now," Tante Vivienne said hurriedly. "Through the kitchen."

So I did not see him. But from the kitchen, I could hear Monsieur Larousse's voice as he entered the house. He sounded cross.

Thursday
7 June

CLAIRE-MARIE WAS SUBDUED today. When I questioned her, she admitted that she had heard her father and mother quarreling last night.

"It was mostly Papa," Claire-Marie said. "Supper did not please him and he was very tired. He works too hard."

"Was he sharp with you?" I asked.

"Oh no," Claire-Marie said, smiling. "He told me I am more beautiful than ever. And he brought me a new French bonnet with yellow feathers. No matter how tired Papa is, he would never be sharp with *me*."

Friday
8 June

TODAY I BOUGHT yellow feathers at the market and stitched them to my gray silk bonnet. But when I snipped the thread, I also cut the fabric across the brim. Horrified, I ran to Maman.

She glanced at the bonnet and said, "Why did you want those gaudy feathers in the first place?"

"All the French bonnets have feathers this season," I said. "But now it's ruined. May I have a new bonnet, Maman? One with feathers?"

"Your papa spends too much on finery for you."

"But Maman, how can I wear the bonnet in this condition?" I cried.

"You like these feathers so much, sew on more to cover the damage," she said. "It couldn't look worse than it does now."

How cruel she can be! But I know when she cannot be reasoned with, so I set about adding three more feathers.

When I tried the bonnet on, the feathers drooped into my eyes. I could not even see without blowing them aside! I caught sight of myself in Maman's looking glass, and it appeared that a great yellow bird had attacked my head and refused to let go.

I thought about wearing the bonnet to Mass tomorrow, and how remorseful Maman would be if I walked blindly into the path of an oncoming cart. But since I do not wish to be either a laughingstock or dead, I have decided instead to give the bonnet to the poor, who cannot afford to be particular.

Saturday
9 June

TONIGHT I HEARD Maman discussing me with Papa. I had not intended to eavesdrop. I was only passing by their chamber when I heard my name—at which point, I stopped to polish the doorknob and happened to hear the rest of the conversation.

She called me "spoiled." However can she say that, with all the work I do for her? The silver would be *black* if not for me! And she said it was time to think about my future.

Papa said, "We have years to plan Simone's future. She is only twelve."

"Thirteen," Maman said, "although I do not wonder that you think her younger. Her behavior is certainly childish enough."

"Give her time, Delphine. She will be a woman long enough, and she has but a little time left to be a child."

"See how you indulge her!" Maman exclaimed.

"What would you have me do?" Papa asked. "Marry her off at thirteen?"

"Certainly not! But we should begin to think about suitable prospects and discuss them with Simone. She must learn that she has responsibilities. She cannot remain a thoughtless, willful child forever."

"I think of Simone as lively, not willful," Papa said. I could hear the smile in his voice. How I loved him for defending me!

"*However* you think of her, she is growing up. I will make a list of suitable young men and bring it to you."

"Very well, Delphine," Papa said.

But it is *not* very well with me! What difference is there between Maman's list of suitable young men and the quadroon balls? Either way, Claire-Marie and I are to be sold off like pigs at market!

Monday
11 June

I TOLD MADELON that Maman is talking of arranging a marriage for me, and Madelon asked what I would prefer. I thought about this but could not decide *what* I prefer. Perhaps not to think of marriage for years and years. Or...

"I could go to France with you," I said. I cannot say which one of us was more surprised by my words. I have thought how lovely it would be to see Paris, of course, but I never dreamed of actually going.

"I cannot come between you and your mother," Madelon said. "But I do understand your predicament. It is not so different from the one I faced as a girl."

"Then may I go with you?" I felt excitement building inside me. Why *shouldn't* I go to Paris? Maman herself said that I am no longer a child.

"Is that what you really wish to do?" Madelon asked. "You should not make a decision this important because you are angry with your mother. Give it some thought. Make certain this is what you really want. Then we will talk."

I do not have to give it more thought. When Madelon returns to Paris, I will go with her.

Tuesday 12 June

THERE WILL BE no drawing lesson tomorrow, because Madelon is entertaining guests! How long has it been since visitors were received in that old house? I asked Madelon who would be there.

"A few artists who know my husband's work and admire it," Madelon said. "I have missed the conversation of artists."

I suppose I cannot begrudge her this one afternoon, but why could she not have planned her gathering on a day when we did not have a lesson?

Thursday
14 June

CLAIRE-MARIE TOLD ME that Madelon borrowed Eulalie yesterday to serve at her party. When Claire-Marie questioned her, Eulalie was eager to discuss the affair.

Six men were there. They discussed art and praised Madelon's husband, except for one man, who seemed to know little about art, Eulalie said. He was a white Américain! And he talked of a newspaper article he was writing. Eulalie said he spoke at length about the cruelty of slavery, and the others agreed with him. Then Madelon introduced the topic of slaves rebelling against their masters, and a lively discussion ensued.

Claire-Marie was shocked. In truth, I am somewhat

shocked myself. It is against the law for people of color to speak of slave rebellion. I do not wish to see Madelon arrested!

Friday
15 June

AT OUR LESSON today, Claire-Marie asked Madelon if she enjoyed entertaining the artists. Madelon looked happy and replied that it was very pleasant. Then Claire-Marie asked if only artists were there.

Madelon studied Claire-Marie's face for a moment; then she smiled. "Eulalie has been indiscreet, I see. But there is no reason why my nieces should not know about my guests."

So she told us about a journalist who has come to New Orleans from Chicago to write a series of articles on slavery for his newspaper. Madelon says it is to be an exposé on the barbaric treatment of slaves in the South. The journalist's name is John Mayfield, and he is renting a house from Julia Bernadin's father, of all people! It is the Bernadins' old summer house outside the city.

"Is Monsieur Mayfield advocating slave revolt?" Claire-Marie asked.

"*Revolt* is a strong word," Madelon said carefully.

"You know it is illegal for the *gens de couleur* to discuss such things."

"But John Mayfield is white."

"*Oui,* but my other friends are not," Madelon said firmly. "Nor are we."

And that is where the conversation ended.

Saturday
16 June

TODAY I WAS subjected to another visit with Grand-père Jules. Thankfully, it was brief. I could see at once that his condition has deteriorated. When Véronique gave him his medicine, she had to lift his head from the pillows. But he had strength enough to eat a bit of the baked apples Maman had brought and complain that they were too tart. The cat sniffed at the apples and backed away with lips curled.

Maman told me to go downstairs and wait while she sat with Grand-père. I was more than happy to obey. The cat followed me.

I searched for Madelon but could not find her. Véronique was in the kitchen making turtle soup. The cat sat down at Véronique's feet and fixed his eyes on the turtle meat she was slicing.

"Grand-père is weaker," I said.

Véronique did not reply.

"What will happen to you and Bodin when he dies?"

"We will be freed on the day of his death."

"That is wonderful!" I exclaimed.

"When slaves are freed, they must leave Louisiana," Véronique said softly. "New Orleans is my home. Where else am I supposed to go?"

"But why must you leave?"

"That is the law. Perhaps the whites fear what freed slaves would do."

"It is wrong to make you go," I said, not understanding this law that forced people to leave the only home they had ever known.

Véronique turned back to her work and did not reply.

I watched her chop the terrapin into small pieces. After a moment, she said, "It is worse for Bodin. When Monsieur Jules dies, Bodin will be without a home *and* grieving."

The cat still sat at Véronique's feet, waiting patiently for a bite of the turtle meat.

"What will happen to the cat?" I asked.

"*Pardon?*"

"When Grand-père dies," I said, "who will care for the cat?"

Véronique shrugged. "I only know it will not be me."

I thought about our conversation as Maman and I walked home. I do not know if Maman will grieve for Grand-père Jules. I think Tante Vivienne will not. And I cannot lie and say that *I* will grieve for my grandfather. It is sad that a man will be missed by no one but his manservant. And sadder still that Véronique and Bodin must leave the city in order to be free.

Tuesday 19 June

A TERRIBLE THING has happened!

Claire-Marie did not meet me to walk to school yesterday. Neither was she there when I arrived. I worried all morning, and when we were at last released, I ran to her house.

I knocked and knocked on the door. Eulalie finally responded to my frantic pounding. I saw at once that she was distraught—and very relieved to see me.

"*Mon Dieu*, I am glad you are here, mam'selle," she cried. "Paulette wished to go for Missy Delphine but feared leaving me alone."

"Whatever has happened, Eulalie? Is someone ill?"

"Worse than that," Eulalie said. Then she told me that a man had brought a letter early that morning.

When Tante Vivienne read it, she sank to the floor, sobbing. Claire-Marie ran to her, begging to know what was wrong. When Tante Vivienne did not respond, my cousin picked up the letter and read it herself. Then she, too, sank to the floor, but she did not cry. Eulalie says she sat there staring at the letter and looking as though all life had drained from her body.

"Who was the letter from?" I demanded.

"Monsieur Larousse," Eulalie said. "Missy Vivienne was wailing that he was not coming back. That is all I know."

Not coming back? I could not believe this! Claire-Marie's papa loves her so dearly, why would he ever desert her?

Tante Vivienne and Claire-Marie had locked themselves in their chambers. They would not respond to my pleas to open the door. In great fear, I ran home and told Maman what had happened. She returned with me to my aunt's house at once.

At first, Tante Vivienne would not answer Maman, either. But finally she unlocked the door and Maman disappeared inside.

Later

MONSIEUR LAROUSSE HAS indeed left Tante Vivienne and Claire-Marie. He said in the letter that he has many debts—gambling debts, Tante Vivienne admitted to Maman—and is in danger of losing his plantation. He can no longer afford to support two families.

Maman says that Tante Vivienne owns her house and its furnishings. When Monsieur Larousse visited, he left enough money to last for three or four months, if they are careful. But he said in the letter that he can do nothing more for them.

I returned to the house twice today, but Claire-Marie remains locked in her chamber and will not see me. Eulalie says she unlocks the door only to accept trays of food, which she barely touches, and she will not speak to anyone.

Wednesday 20 June

MAMAN INSISTS THAT I go to school, but I cannot concentrate on lessons. The girls were desperate to know where Claire-Marie was. I have told them and Madame Sardou that my cousin is ill and will not be returning to school for a while. Madame accepted my explanation, but I fear my classmates do not believe me. Especially Gisèle Dubois, who has always enjoyed hearing of others' misfortunes. Minette has been kind. She wrote a letter wishing Claire-Marie well and asked me to deliver it.

Claire-Marie still will not speak to anyone.

Thursday
21 June

AT LAST! CLAIRE-MARIE opened her door when I knocked this afternoon. She was so unkempt, I could not believe this was my beautiful cousin!

She wears the same dress she wore the day the letter arrived. It is badly wrinkled and stained with food. Her hair is tangled, and her eyes are red and swollen. I did not know what to say to her. I could only hold her and murmur endearments while she clung to me and cried.

Later

MAMAN BARELY LEAVES Tante Vivienne's side. She comes home to bathe and see that the house is running smoothly, then returns to her sister. Papa understands.

Maman sent a message to Madelon early in the week

to tell her what has happened. She also said that I would not be coming for my lessons until Claire-Marie has improved. We have heard nothing in response.

Friday 22 June

TODAY MAMAN TOLD Eulalie to heat water and fill the copper tub. Maman helped Tante Vivienne with her bath, fixed her hair, and found a fresh gown for her to wear. Tante Vivienne still does nothing except cry, but Maman persuaded her to eat some sliced peaches and crawfish bisque. Tante Vivienne weeps and says that she could not go on without her dear sister.

Claire-Marie also agreed to bathe, and I combed the tangles from her hair. But when I brought out the dress with the embroidered roses on it, she collapsed on her bed in tears. This was what she wore the last time she saw her papa. I found her white muslin and she permitted me to help her dress.

Later

MAMAN PREPARED A light supper for Tante Vivienne and Claire-Marie—cold turkey, cheese, cakes, and tea. My aunt and cousin are slowly regaining their appetites, but still they are so miserable! Maman says it is not my place to judge Monsieur Larousse, but I cannot help but think he is the most detestable man alive!

Saturday
23 June

CLAIRE-MARIE AGREED TO go outside for some exercise this afternoon. The air was close and damp, and soon our dresses were clinging to our backs, but walking around the courtyard seemed to soothe my cousin's mind. She did not cry once.

Soon after we went inside, Madelon arrived. She went over to Claire-Marie and held her close while murmuring words I could not hear. Then Claire-Marie began to weep, but I could see that Madelon's presence brought my cousin comfort.

Madelon stayed for supper and was very gentle with Tante Vivienne. She said she had waited to visit, fearing that Vivienne would not want her there.

"But you and Claire-Marie have been in my thoughts and prayers every moment," Madelon said. "My heart breaks for you."

I was surprised when Tante Vivienne embraced Madelon. They both cried as they held each other.

I am very tired, but I cannot sleep. My mind is filled

with concern for my aunt and cousin. Whatever will become of them?

Sunday 24 June

ST. JOHN'S DAY. Madame Sardou says they celebrate this day in Europe by lighting bonfires and dancing and feasting and drinking until they reel. In New Orleans, we recognize the day by attending Mass.

If I were Saint John, I would celebrate my day in Europe.

Evening

GRAND-PÈRE GROWS WEAKER. He slips in and out of a deep sleep from which no one can rouse him. Maman sent for Papa and my brothers, and we hurried to Grand-père's house.

When Bodin let us in, I searched his face. If he grieves, it does not show.

Madelon sat beside Grand-père's bed. She held his hand and stroked his hair. When we entered the room, she said softly, "He is awake. I know he will be happy you came."

Maman and Papa approached the bed. Madelon

rose, as though to give Maman her chair, but Grand-père grabbed for Madelon's hand and looked distressed.

"Stay," he whispered to Madelon.

She sank into the chair again and murmured, "Of course I will stay, Papa. Delphine and I will be here, never fear."

The cat lay at Grand-père's side, his eyes following us. He seemed to be standing guard.

Later, in the drawing room, Madelon said, "The doctor says he could go on this way for weeks. Or he could slip away in a moment."

"He has forgiven you," Maman said. She sounded pleased.

"*Oui,* he has," Madelon replied, and her eyes filled with tears. "*Merci,* sister, for giving me the chance to make amends."

Then they spoke of Tante Vivienne and Claire-Marie.

"We must tell them about Papa," Madelon said. "But I thought you should be the one, Delphine. Is Vivienne composed enough to visit him?"

"I will see her when we leave here," Maman said. "No matter how great her sorrow over Monsieur Larousse, she would never forgive herself if she did not see Papa before he dies."

"*C'est mal,*" Madelon said softly. "It is very bad

what that man did, but can Vivienne be surprised? Surely she must have known this could happen to her, as it has to so many others."

"Perhaps she could not bear to think of it," Maman replied.

"At least," Madelon said thoughtfully, "Claire-Marie can be saved."

"Saved?" Maman's expression was puzzled.

"She will not be going to the balls after all. How could she wish to now?"

"But Claire-Marie has been prepared for no other life," Maman said. "I think once she has recovered from this sorrow, she will go to the balls as Vivienne planned."

"Surely not!" Madelon exclaimed. "Would she wish to live her mother's life after seeing what can happen?"

Maman shrugged. "But what else is there for Claire-Marie? She will not marry a man of color. The life of a craftsman's wife would be intolerable to her."

Maman said this in front of Papa and my brothers. I wondered what they were thinking, but their faces told me nothing.

Papa stayed at Grand-père's house with Maman, so it was left to me to prepare a hasty meal for my brothers and myself. Fruit and cheese were all I could manage.

"No soup?" Gabi asked as he sat down and surveyed the table. "No meat?"

"There wasn't time to cook," I said defensively.

"This is women's fare," Gabi grumbled. "Men need a hearty meal."

"You ate enough for three men at dinner," I informed him. "Otherwise, there would be gumbo left for tonight."

My normally placid and accommodating brother found fault with everything I served. The cheese was hard. The melon was green. I had no skill in the kitchen; thus, my future as a wife was questionable.

Tin-Tin looked ready to leap to my defense, but I did not give him the chance. With fire in my eyes, I turned to Gabi and said, "Could it be that I have no interest in cooking? That I do not even *wish* to marry the likes of you? I ask you, Gabriel, what kind of life can a man of color give me? Perhaps Claire-Marie is wise to eschew that prospect."

As soon as I had uttered the words, I was sorry. Gabi's expression did not change except for the tightening of his jaw, but Tin-Tin looked surprised, then hurt.

"Are you saying that you are too good to marry a man like our father?" Gabi asked in a cold voice.

"No," I replied hastily. "I did not mean—"

"But you did mean it," Gabi interrupted. "And who can blame you? As you said, what kind of life can a man of color give you? Do you not think I would have a different life if I could? If Papa would allow it? Do you think I enjoy acting the humble servant whenever a white man enters the studio? Saying, '*Oui,* monsieur' and '*Non,* monsieur' while they address me as Gabriel, as though I were a child?"

"Gabi, I'm sorry," I said miserably. "I did not mean it. Honestly. This wretched temper of mine takes over, and I lose whatever sense I have. I would be honored to marry a man like Papa, or like my brothers. Truly, Gabi."

His face relaxed and he patted my hand. "I, too, am sorry," he said wearily. "You will make some man the best of wives. But it will not be an easy life, little sister. Not in this city. Not with a man of color."

He left soon after for the taverns.

"Don't worry, Simone," Tin-Tin said kindly. "By the fourth drink, he will have forgotten what you said."

"And will you forget also, Tin-Tin?"

"It is forgotten already."

"Sometimes I can be as thoughtless as Claire-Marie!" I chided myself.

"I think not," he said cheerfully. "You would have to work very hard to be *that* thoughtless."

As he often does, Tin-Tin made me smile. But I was still worrying about Gabi.

"Gabi drinks too much," I said.

"I don't understand why he cannot be content with our life here," Tin-Tin replied. "It is a *good* life, Simone. Surely there are difficulties wherever one lives."

I suppose that is true. But if Gabi were to live in Paris, he would be addressed as Monsieur Racine. A small thing, but I understand its importance to him.

"Do you not ever want more than you have?" I asked Tin-Tin.

"Never," he replied. "What more is there to want?"

Monday 25 June

I ACCOMPANIED TANTE Vivienne and Claire-Marie to Grand-père's house. Maman and Madelon took them upstairs to see Grand-père. Claire-Marie stayed only a few moments, then joined me in the courtyard.

"He was asleep," she said. "The deep sleep Madelon told us about."

Claire-Marie sat down beside me on the edge of the fountain. Her hair was brushed and her dress was clean. Dark smudges lay beneath her eyes, but the redness from weeping was gone.

"It is just as Maman feared," Claire-Marie said wearily. "Madelon has been embraced by Grand-père.

Maman says he called in his lawyer last week, no doubt to change his will in favor of Madelon."

"We do not know that."

"*I* know," Claire-Marie said. "But I do not blame Madelon. How can I? She is everything you said, Simone. She asks for nothing from Grand-père, but he will give her everything. And Maman will receive nothing."

"Whatever happens, Tante Vivienne will be fine," I said. "She has a comfortable home and she is still young and beautiful."

"But not young enough to find another protector," Claire-Marie replied. "*Oui*, she has a house and pretty gowns and French furnishings. But you cannot eat a chair, Simone. We have no choice but to sell the best furniture, and Maman will rent out rooms." Then she added defensively, "She must do *something* to put food on the table."

Claire-Marie's words filled my heart with sadness. I cannot imagine my proud, carefree aunt renting rooms in her home to strangers! Or counting her pennies and worrying if there will be enough to see her through the week.

"Is there not another way?" I asked.

"She could marry a butcher," Claire-Marie replied sharply. "Or a barber, or a cigar maker. Would that be a better way, Simone?"

I realized then that Tante Vivienne and Claire-Marie would prefer almost any life to the one my mother and I live. I wanted to weep.

Tuesday
26 June

CLAIRE-MARIE WILL NOT return to school. She says Tante Vivienne can no longer afford to send her. But since tuition has been paid through the term, I assume that Claire-Marie is simply too ashamed to face our classmates.

Maman has taken charge of arranging to sell Tante Vivienne's furniture. My aunt cannot bear to part with anything and bursts into tears when Maman suggests selling so much as a footstool. Claire-Marie avoids the issue by leaving the house whenever such matters are being discussed. I do not know where she goes.

Later

THIS AFTERNOON CLAIRE-MARIE came downstairs, to find Paulette wrapping silver spoons in soft cloths while Maman added them to her list. The silver is to be auctioned along with the furniture. I heard Maman tell Papa that Claire-Marie looked shocked when she saw what they were doing. Then she became angry and screamed that they were not to take the tea service that her father had given to Tante Vivienne. Maman tried to calm her, but Claire-Marie ran from the house crying, "I cannot stay here!"

Wednesday 27 June

EVERYONE KNOWS THAT Monsieur Larousse has left Tante Vivienne. Some of the girls at school are nasty about it—the same ones who used to trot after Claire-Marie like pet dogs. I heard Gisèle Dubois say to Julia Bernadin that Claire-Marie has always acted as though she is better than everyone else, and now she is getting what she deserves. Julia agreed. Only Minette and Silvie Renan seem to feel sympathy for Claire-Marie. And of course Silvie would, since the same thing happened to her mother.

Claire-Marie no longer wishes to attend our painting lessons, so I go alone.

Thursday 28 June

I DREW MORE scenes of Congo Square from memory. I sketched women with their skirts billowing as they danced, revealing their shapely legs above the knee. I drew the children, barely clothed, with bits of ribbon in their hair. Madame Sardou would be scandalized!

Friday 29 June

MADELON WAS SO preoccupied, she scarcely spoke to me while I sketched an arrangement of books and wine bottles. She must be worried about Grand-père. And of course Tante Vivienne.

When I could stand the silence no longer, I said, "I understand now why you left New Orleans. I have thought about it, as you said I should, and have decided to go to Paris with you."

Madelon had been staring out the window. When I spoke, she turned to me with a puzzled expression.

"You said I should give it more thought—"

"Not now, Simone," Madelon said. "There will be time to discuss Paris later."

"But you *will* let me go with you," I said, suddenly fearful that she did not want me.

"I cannot think about that now," Madelon replied impatiently. "In fact, why don't we end the lesson early today? There are things I must do."

She left the room before I could respond.

I know that Madelon is not herself these days. I should be more tolerant of her behavior, because she must carry a great burden of sorrow as her papa lies dying. But still, I am hurt by her dismissal. Could she not have taken a moment to say, Of course you will go to Paris with me, Simone. Was that ever in question?

Evening

I LOOKED THROUGH my dresses to choose what I will take to Paris. The new Chinese crepe, of course, and my other best frocks. But I will leave my school dresses behind.

Tin-Tin saw me holding up dresses in front of Maman's looking glass and asked what I was doing. After making him promise not to tell anyone, I shared my secret with him. He appeared stunned.

"But Simone, what will we do without you here? And what will Maman say?"

I shrugged. “I will not be around to hear her.”

Tin-Tin frowned. “That sounds like something Claire-Marie would say, not you.”

“Why does everyone think I am so different from Claire-Marie?” I asked crossly.

“Because you are,” my brother said. “Besides, why would you wish to leave your family? You know it would break Papa’s heart.”

Madelon’s words came back to me then and I found myself saying, “If I remain here, I will be living Papa and Maman’s life, not my own.”

“And what is wrong with their life?” Tin-Tin asked, studying my face with worried eyes.

“Every day is the same,” I replied. “Maman cares for the house, plans the meals, visits Grand-père. Papa goes to the studio, comes home for dinner, goes back to the studio. Do you not see how monotonous their days are? There is no passion—no excitement in their lives, only responsibility and duty.”

“Excitement,” Tin-Tin repeated thoughtfully. “As there is in Tante Madelon’s life, you mean.”

“Exactly!” I exclaimed. “Madelon is not afraid to live as she pleases. She will not be bound by the opinions and expectations of others.”

“*Oui,* it does seem that Tante Madelon’s life has been about things other than responsibility and duty,”

Tin-Tin agreed. "But where would you and Gabi and I be if Papa and Maman had ignored their duty to us?"

"You aren't in a position to judge Madelon," I said sharply. "You don't even know her."

"How well do *you* know her?" Tin-Tin demanded.

Growing weary of the conversation, I turned away and began to fold my dress for packing. Even though I was critical of Madelon myself only a short time ago, I do not want to hear anyone else criticize her. And I do understand her character better than Tin-Tin does.

Before he left, my brother said, "I hope you will change your mind about going."

But I will not.

July 1838

Sunday
1 July

WHEN I WENT to Claire-Marie's house this afternoon, I could not believe the changes. The drawing room carpet was rolled up and tied with cord. The piano and many of the paintings were gone. Even the bedchambers had been stripped to the bare essentials: bed, armoire, table, chamber pot. Claire-Marie and Tante Vivienne were resting, so after wandering through the sad, silent house, I joined Eulalie in the kitchen. She was eager to tell me that she had served Madelon's guests again.

"There were more this time," Eulalie said. "All men of color except for that white writer. But I cannot repeat what I heard," she added in a hushed voice.

Her coyness irritated me, but I was too curious to reprimand her. "I will not tell anyone," I assured her.

Eulalie was easily persuaded. She said that John Mayfield talked about helping slaves escape from their masters. He believes it is the moral thing to do. And Madelon agreed with him. I certainly will not repeat this to anyone, because I do not wish to see my aunt confined like a common criminal. But I do wish she would have nothing more to do with this white Américain!

Monday
2 July

I AM WEARY of drawing. And even more, I am weary of waiting. I do not wish to hasten Grand-père's death, but while he lives, Madelon and I are obliged to remain here. Now that I know what I wish to do, I am impatient to *do* it!

Wednesday
4 July

CLAIRE-MARIE SAYS THAT Paulette and Eulalie are to be sold! I said that she must be mistaken, and Claire-Marie replied, "We have no money to feed slaves. Besides, they are young and strong. They will bring a good price." She said this in such a cold, matter-of-fact way, I realized that I do not even *know* my cousin any longer. She grew up with Paulette and Eulalie. Does it cause her no pain to picture them on the slave block?

Later

MAMAN SAYS THAT Paulette and Eulalie will be sold after the house is cleaned and the rooms prepared for boarders. Tante Vivienne will not let them go until all the heavy work is finished. My aunt has them working in the courtyard today because she does not wish to pay a gardener. Maman says that Paulette and Eulalie are trimming trees and bushes in the best of spirits—for they do not yet know the fate that awaits them! My heart aches for them.

Thursday
5 July

IF ONLY I were a man, so that I could swear and spit! Today I thought to settle Paulette's and Eulalie's future by speaking with Maman. I suggested that Papa purchase the girls from Tante Vivienne and save them from the slave auction. But before I could present my arguments, Maman said, "Absolutely not. One servant is all we need."

I tried to reason with her, but she would not hear it! So I went to Papa's studio to speak with him.

Papa was with a customer when I arrived—a Creole named LaGrange. I have seen this man often around the city with his plump wife and pretty daughters.

"I paid you half when I commissioned the work," Monsieur LaGrange was saying. "I will pay the rest now."

"*Pardon*, monsieur," Papa said in the soft, polite

voice he uses with white men. "But my records show you paid only a quarter."

"Then your records are incorrect," the man said curtly. "I remember distinctly giving you half." He withdrew money from his coat pocket and handed it to Papa. "I consider my account paid in full."

"Monsieur, the statue of St. Joseph was unusually elaborate. The marble had to be specially ordered; it cost me more—"

"And your work was excellent," Monsieur LaGrange replied as he strode toward the door. "*Au revoir*, Jean-Louis."

When he was gone, Gabi said, "Papa, he *did* pay only a quarter. I was here when he commissioned the statue."

"We know that and so does he." Papa counted the money. "This barely covers the cost of the marble."

"You must go to his home and insist that he pay the rest," Gabi said.

"That would be useless," Papa replied. "It is his word against ours. He will not pay."

"Then we will take him to court!" Tin-Tin cried. "We will sue him for the rest."

"You know better than that," Papa said. "Men of color cannot testify against whites in court."

"Then what will we do?" Gabi mumbled.

"We will be too busy to do any more work for Monsieur LaGrange," Papa said.

Then he saw me standing there. Without so much as a hello, Papa said, "You know your mother does not want you here."

I had not arrived at a good time. But I was there, so I told him why I had come. Papa regarded me with a stern expression—something I am not accustomed to from him.

"You have a tender heart, Ti-Simone, and that pleases me," he said, not looking pleased at all. "But this idea is impossible. You cannot help every negro in New Orleans."

"But I only wish to help Paulette and Eulalie."

"I haven't the money," he said, turning back to his work. "Now hurry home before your mother misses you."

"But Papa—"

"Go home, Simone."

Tin-Tin's expression was sympathetic, but Gabi looked as though he thought I had taken leave of my senses.

When I arrived home, I came straight away to my chamber. Maman looked in a moment ago and I expected her to chastise me about work I had left undone. Instead, she said in a surprisingly gentle voice, "I, too, regret that Paulette and Eulalie must be sold, but your aunt cannot afford to keep them."

"Papa could buy them if he were willing," I said.

"But do you not see how that would shame Vivienne?" Maman asked. She left before I could argue.

The house is filled with mosquitoes, so I sit on my bed to write with the netting pulled down. Since I did not think to remove my slippers, the blue coverlet is white with stone dust. It is also splattered with ink.

Perhaps I will be in Paris before Maman notices.

Friday
6 July

YESTERDAY I WENT to the storeroom and found a large valise. It is hidden beneath my bed and I pack odds and ends as I think of them.

My recitations are so terrible, Madame Sardou threatens to expel me. She and the girls appear surprised that I do not seem to care.

I am still angry with everyone who will not help Paulette and Eulalie. I speak when I am spoken to and that is all.

At dinner, Maman said, "The bouillabaisse is excellent, Simone. You are becoming quite accomplished with your cooking."

"*Merci*, Maman," I replied, not looking up from the table.

"And the mirliton is so tender," she added.

"*Merci*, Maman."

"You have been working so hard, I think you deserve something special," Maman said then. I did not look at her, but I could see Gabi's and Tin-Tin's shocked expressions across the table. They were as surprised by Maman's kindness toward me as I was.

"What would you like?" Maman asked. "A new bonnet, perhaps? One with yellow feathers like your cousin's?"

"*Merci*, Maman," I said politely, "but I think not. Do you not agree that the feathers are somewhat gaudy?"

When I looked at her, Maman was frowning. Later, I overheard her complaining to Papa.

"Simone did not seem rude to me," he was saying. "In fact, she was extremely polite, I thought."

"Exactly!" Maman exclaimed. "She was *so* polite, she was rude. Surely you could see that!"

Papa sighed. "Delphine, I do not understand what you are talking about."

"She has been spending too much time with Madelon," Maman continued. "Even though Madelon is my sister, I would not want Simone to emulate her."

"I think you are worrying needlessly," Papa replied. "And I haven't time to discuss it now. I must return to work."

Maman is still upset. I am feeling better, but *ma mère*'s concern has set me to wondering: Could it be that she is jealous of my closeness to Madelon?

Saturday 7 July

LAST EVENING AFTER supper, Maman went to the kitchen, which she usually does not do. I thought I knew why she was going, so I followed her and stood outside the door to listen.

When she told Azura that Paulette and Eulalie are to be sold at the slave auction, there was a brief silence. Then a terrible sound filled the air—a wail of such anguish, I felt ashamed to be eavesdropping. So I crept upstairs to my chamber, where I could cry in private.

Later, when I went downstairs for a slice of cake left from supper, I heard Papa's voice coming from his and Maman's chamber.

"*Calme-toi*, Delphine," he was saying. "You will make yourself ill if you carry on so."

I was surprised enough by the tenderness in his voice,

and *astounded* by the muffled sobs coming from behind their door.

I have never seen Maman weep. It is unimaginable.

Later

MADELON DID NOT know about Paulette and Eulalie until I told her. Finally, someone else is as indignant as I am.

"I cannot believe my sister would do this, no matter what her circumstances," Madelon said. "When, Simone? When are they taking the girls to auction?"

"Not until Tante Vivienne has gotten the last ounce of blood from them," I said. "Maman says they are making coverlets for the boarders' beds today."

"Then perhaps there is time," Madelon said softly.

"Time for what?"

"To get Paulette and Eulalie away from here."

"You mean help them run away?"

"Why do you look so shocked?" she demanded.

"Helping slaves—helping them escape is—it is against the law," I stammered.

"Selling and keeping slaves is worse," Madelon said. Then she sighed. "I forget that you are only a child, Simone. Never mind what I said."

"But—"

"Just go home," Madelon said. "There are things I must do."

Those who help runaway slaves are severely punished. Especially people of color. Why would Madelon risk everything to help people she barely knows? Why would she risk everything while Maman will risk nothing? I am frightened for Madelon.

Much later

I CANNOT SLEEP. It is unbearably hot and mosquitoes buzz incessantly, as does my head. Madelon's words still make me tremble, although I cannot help but admire her courage.

Sunday 8 July

LATE LAST NIGHT I went to Tin-Tin's chamber. We climbed out to the roof and watched people come to Azura for her *voudou*. She turned them all away. They pleaded, but she shook her head violently and shut the door in their faces. Even so, I could see candles burning on the floor of the cottage and bottles filled with her magic powders on the table. Azura may be sending customers away, but she is still making *voudou*. Against Tante Vivienne, no doubt. Perhaps the rest of us, as well.

Which means I will not be eating Azura's cooking in the foreseeable future.

Tante Vivienne and Claire-Marie no longer attend Mass. Today I saw Henri Jourdan watching another young woman who was strolling the place d'Armes. She was not so pretty as Claire-Marie, but she had light skin and a lively manner.

After dinner, I accompanied Maman to Grand-père's house. While Maman went upstairs to see him, I stayed with Madelon. I told her I wanted to help.

"Help with what?"

"Paulette and Eulalie. Do you have a plan for getting them out of New Orleans?"

Madelon looked surprised. She glanced over her shoulder, as though fearing someone had overheard.

"Let us go out to the courtyard," she said quickly.

Once outside, she said, "Now, what are you talking about?"

"Paulette's and Eulalie's escape," I said. "Everything you said is true. Selling Paulette and Eulalie at the auction is wrong. I want to help them run away."

"That is very brave of you, *chérie*," Madelon said carefully. "But you are still a child."

"*Non*," I said firmly. "Even Maman says I am not.

She says it is time for me to behave as a woman. Does that not mean doing what I know to be right?"

Madelon studied my face, considering. Then she nodded. "*Oui*, that is what it means," she replied. "But you could be putting yourself at risk, Simone. If your mother should find out..."

"That does not matter," I replied. My heart was beating hard against my ribs. I was frightened, but also excited.

"There is someone who will help us," Madelon said.

"John Mayfield, the Américain."

Madelon smiled. "You miss nothing, do you, little niece?" she demanded. "*Oui*, John Mayfield will help. But you must not mention his name to anyone."

"Where will he take them?"

"To another man some miles from the city, who will take them to another, and so on," Madelon said. "People all along the way will help Paulette and Eulalie reach Canada."

"Canada!"

"Hush," Madelon said softly. "No one must hear us. But, yes, Simone, they will go to Canada, where they can be free."

Monday
9 July

A MOST DISTURBING day! While Maman went to see Tante Vivienne and Claire-Marie, I helped Azura prepare dinner for Papa and my brothers. Azura was clearly in a wretched mood, banging pots and muttering under her breath. I do not question Azura about her moods for fear she will sprinkle powdered worms or lizard eyes into my soup, although I could not help but hear some of what she said. And it was enough to make my head ache and my hand tremble!

She mumbled as she worked that the south wind would scorch their bodies and make them wither, and the north wind would freeze their blood and numb their limbs; the west wind would blow away their life's breath, and the east wind would darken their sight. They would lose their hair and their bones would crumble to dust. Their ears would fall off and their skin would rot. She muttered all this, as well as other sickening predictions, while chopping peppers with Maman's sharpest knife! It was all I could do to stay and listen.

Then she seemed to pray—though not to any God I know—asking that disease and death visit her enemies, that their crops not prosper and their animals perish from starvation and thirst, that their homes collapse and floods wash them away, that their wombs shrivel and drop from their bodies.

This was truly more than I could bear. I blurted out that I was feeling unwell and ran from the kitchen. Surely even Maman could not fault me for refusing to stir gumbo this day!

Later

MADELON HAS BOUGHT Paulette and Eulalie time by telling Tante Vivienne that she needs them to clean Grand-père's house. Since so many rooms have been closed and untended during his illness, Tante Vivienne did not question this. But she told Madelon that she needs money and cannot wait long to sell them. Madelon offered to pay for the girls' time and Tante Vivienne agreed.

I am to tell Paulette and Eulalie that we will help them escape. They are to go about their work as normally as possible and confide in no one—except Azura, of course, since we know they will tell her in any case.

When John Mayfield has arranged to take them to a safe house, he will give Madelon the word to proceed. On the evening they are to leave, I will take them to

Grand-père's house, where Madelon will be waiting. She will take them to Monsieur Mayfield.

"No one will question you being at your cousin's home," Madelon said. "But after you bring Paulette and Eulalie to me, you must go home at once and be inside before curfew. When Vivienne notices the girls are gone next morning, there will be nothing to connect you with their disappearance."

I told Madelon that I could take them to John Mayfield. "I know a shortcut through the swamp," I said. "People of color cannot leave the city without permission, and if you take the road, you could be seen."

"The authorities do not know me," Madelon said. "If we run into a patrol, all they will see is a white woman traveling with her slaves. Besides, you forget that I grew up here—*I* know shortcuts, as well."

I do not care if Tante Vivienne and Maman find out that I was involved in the girls' disappearance—because very soon I will be leaving New Orleans myself.

Tuesday
10 July

TODAY AFTER SCHOOL, I went to Claire-Marie's house—purportedly to see my cousin but, in fact, to speak to Paulette and Eulalie. I had not seen the sisters since they learned that they are to be sold. When Paulette answered my knock, she looked very tired and sad. And no wonder!

She said that my aunt and cousin were upstairs, and she moved as though to tell them I was there. But I stopped her and said I wished to speak to her and Eulalie.

To say they were cheered by my news is an understatement. "*Merci, merci,*" they said over and over. Eulalie cried tears of relief and gratitude. I told them to behave as they always do—and, for goodness' sake, not to look happy. They promised to appear as gloomy as a man on the way to his hanging.

When I left them, I went to Claire-Marie's chamber. She was lying on the bed fully dressed. I sat down beside her.

"My papa ordered the fabric for this canopy," she said, her eyes fixed on the rose silk overhead. "Surely he must have cared if he ordered silk all the way from France."

"Of course he cared," I replied.

"But still he left," my cousin said softly.

Wednesday 11 July

MADELON HAS HEARD nothing from John Mayfield. I grow more and more fearful when I consider what we are doing.

Grand-père's condition has not changed. I went to his house today for my lesson, but I told Madelon that I did not feel like drawing. We talked a little, but she said it is dangerous to discuss what is uppermost in our minds, so we spoke of everything else.

She told me Grand-père Jules has nightmares. "Last night I heard him screaming," she said. "When I went to his chamber, I found him tossing and twisting in bed. He cried out, '*Dead!* All of them, *dead*!'"

"Was he dreaming about his wife and sons?"

Madelon gave me a sharp look. "What do you know about them?"

"Only that the freed slaves killed them," I said.

"What else do you know about those times?" Madelon asked.

"That they were terrible."

Madelon nodded. "*Oui*, they were terrible. I never think about it myself. Why dwell on misery?"

But something in her face told me that she was not telling the truth.

Thursday
12 July

MAMAN IS WORRIED about Tante Vivienne, who never leaves the house and seems overwhelmed by sorrow. I remember hearing Maman and Tante Vivienne speak of another woman whose protector had left her. The woman was so overcome by grief, she walked to the river, tied a sack of stones around her waist, and jumped into the water. They never found her body. Tin-Tin said the fish probably nibbled away at her until there was nothing left.

I wonder if Maman fears that Tante Vivienne will take a walk to the river.

Friday
13 July

MADELON WAS NOT home when I arrived for my lesson. Véronique did not know where she was. I waited in the kitchen, hoping Madelon would have news for me when she returned.

"How is Grand-père?" I asked Véronique.

"The same," she said. "Bodin is with him now. Bodin believes that even when Monsieur Jules is in the deep sleep, he knows if someone is there."

"Why is Bodin so loyal to Grand-père?" I asked.

Véronique shrugged. "Who can say? Perhaps because Monsieur Jules saved his life."

"But I thought it was Bodin who saved Grand-père's life!"

"*Oui,* in Haiti he did," Véronique replied. "But on the ship coming to New Orleans, Monsieur Jules returned the favor. There was a terrible storm and Bodin fell overboard. He could not swim and would have drowned—except your grandfather dove into the water and held him until the ship's crew could pull them to safety. When they were back on the ship, lying soaked and exhausted on the deck, your grandfather turned to Bodin—and do you know what he said?"

I shook my head.

"Monsieur Jules said, 'Now we are even, Bodin. Do not ever save my life again.'"

"Why would he say that?"

"He did not want to be indebted to Bodin a second time," Véronique replied.

I thought about this and then I said, "Grand-père could have died."

"*Oui,* the ocean was treacherous."

"My grandfather is brave," I said, feeling strangely awed by this discovery.

"He *is* brave," Véronique said. "I have never questioned that. There are many sides to Monsieur Agneau."

Then she shared another of those sides with me. Something Bodin had told her about their escape from Haiti.

"Monsieur Jules, Bodin, and your aunts met a family with young children. They were also trying to escape, and they asked if they might join your grandfather's party. Monsieur Jules agreed. It was late at night. They had to travel a long distance by foot to reach the harbor, where they hoped to bribe a ship's captain into allowing them to stow away. They were in grave danger. They knew if the bands of freed slaves that roamed the countryside were to discover them, they would be killed. When your grandfather and the others saw men coming, they would jump into a ditch and lie flat until the men had passed. One time, they were lying in a ditch and the other family's baby began to whimper. The freed slaves were approaching and Bodin was afraid the baby would start to cry and give them away."

"But the baby did not cry," I said, thinking this was the end of the story.

"No, it did not cry," Véronique replied. "Because your grandfather placed his hands around the baby's throat and squeezed. When the freed slaves passed, they heard no sound because the baby was dead."

So I have learned more about my grandfather. He is brave. And he is terrible—far more terrible than I imagined.

When Madelon still did not return, I left for home. It seems that all I do is wait for her.

Saturday, late
14 July

BASTILLE DAY THE heat was oppressive. Papa and my brothers did not return to the studio after the midday meal, but remained at home, where it was cooler. Even Maman did not feel like working. We closed the shutters and sat in the parlor, fanning ourselves and drinking tamarind juice. Gabi left early for the taverns, saying, "A glass of whiskey will not make me cooler, but it will help me forget the heat."

For supper, we had fruit and cheese. Maman and Papa went to their chamber early. When we were alone, Tin-Tin said, "There is something I want you to see."

I followed him to his chamber and out the window to the roof.

"What is it?" I asked.

"Be patient and you will see," he replied.

We sat and waited until the moon was high in the sky. Azura began to receive people who came to purchase dreams and curses. She no longer turned them away, so I knew that Paulette and Eulalie had spoken with her.

We waited a long time. I was growing tired of wiping the sweat from my face and swatting at mosquitoes. "Nothing is happening," I whispered to Tin-Tin.

"It will," he said softly.

Perhaps a quarter of an hour later, the gate to the courtyard opened and a man entered. When he stepped from the shadows into the moonlight, I gasped—for making his way down the path to Azura's door was Gabi! My own brother had come to the mambo for her *voudou*!

"Tin-Tin—"

"Hush, or he will hear you," Tin-Tin cautioned, but I could detect a hint of amusement in his voice.

"Do you find this entertaining?" I demanded. "Our brother selling his soul to the devil woman for...for— Why *has* he come to see her?"

"For vanity's sake," Tin-Tin said as we watched Azura admit Gabi into her cottage and close the door behind him.

"What are you talking about, Celestin?"

"Gabi's hair," Tin-Tin replied. "Or perhaps I should say, his lack of hair. Have you not noticed how his forehead grows wider and wider? Before long, his head will be as shiny as Papa's."

It is true that Papa has little hair on top, although he has thick sideburns. "But what does that have to do with Azura?" I asked.

"She gives Gabi an ointment to make hair grow," Tin-Tin said. "I came upon him one night when he was using it. *Mon Dieu*, Simone—that salve smells worse than what a mule leaves behind! Gabi must be desperate for hair!"

He said that Gabi mixes boar's grease, ashes from burnt bees, burnt lizard's liver, and spirits of vinegar into a paste. He takes the mixture to Azura, who chants and spits into it to make the magic work. Then he smears the foul mess on his scalp.

I am fortunate to have Maman's thick hair. But should I ever lose it, my head will shine like dew in the morning sun before I resort to boar's grease and Azura's spittle!

Sunday
15 July

ANOTHER LONG MASS. I occupied myself by watching others nod off, then jerk awake and glance around to see if anyone had noticed. My eyes fell on Gabi as he was rubbing his head with his fingertips—feeling for new hair, no doubt. Tin-Tin nudged me, our eyes met, and laughter welled up inside us. We managed to stifle our merriment so that it sounded more like sputtery coughs, but Maman is annoyed just the same. She says I have disgraced her before God and the Heavenly Host. More likely, it is embarrassment before the neighbors that vexes her most.

I am confined to my chamber until I complete a list of my sins. Maman says it will be a long list.

Monday 16 July

STILL NO WORD from John Mayfield.

Maman and Tante Vivienne visited Grand-père today. I was prepared to go with them for my drawing lesson, but Tante Vivienne said that Madelon would be out all afternoon. She had taken Claire-Marie shopping to lift my cousin's spirits. I stayed home, feeling abandoned and out of sorts. No one ever thinks to lift *my* spirits! And why couldn't Madelon have told me she was canceling our lesson? Maman would advise me to add childishness to my list of sins.

Later

MAMAN CAME HOME looking flushed and excited. I could tell she had important news to share, but, of course, she had no intention of sharing it with me. When Maman and Papa retired to their chamber after supper, I followed and stood outside the door to listen. It is Maman's fault that I am reduced to such deceitful practices.

What I heard is this: Grand-père is not leaving his house to Madelon. He told Tante Vivienne today that the house and furnishings, his carriage, and the horses will all be hers. Maman said Tante Vivienne looked much relieved and actually smiled. She embraced Grand-père and showered him with tears until he brushed her aside, demanding that she give a dying man some peace.

Madelon and Claire-Marie returned soon after. Tante Vivienne was still weeping. One look at her and Madelon concluded that Grand-père had left this life—until Tante Vivienne exclaimed, "Oh no, dear sister, Papa is still with us," and proceeded to explain the reason for her show of emotion. Maman said Madelon looked shocked when she heard that Tante Vivienne would inherit Grand-père's estate. And Tante Vivienne behaved badly. Maman said she was gloating, although she professed grief over the prospect of losing Grand-père.

"I wonder if Madelon *did* expect to inherit," Maman said to Papa. "She certainly appeared disappointed to learn otherwise."

I do not believe this. What need does Madelon have for a house in New Orleans when she already has one in Paris?

Another thought: Even if Maman was forced to marry Papa against her will, she has come to rely on him more than I had realized.

Tuesday 17 July

I WENT TO the market because Azura forgot to get peppers. As I wandered through the crowd, it suddenly occurred to me that I will miss the sights and sounds of New Orleans when I leave for France. The people in all shades of brown, white, yellow, red, and black. The voices bartering in French and English, Spanish and Greek. The smells of coffee, fish, oranges, and cloves. I do not want to forget any part of it! Not the taste of cakes flavored with honey, nor the shouts of wagon drivers to their horses, nor the clatter of carts filled with cabbages and apples, nor the screech of parrots in their cages. As I watched and listened, I felt such an overwhelming sense of loss that tears sprang to my eyes. I have only just realized how much I love New Orleans. I will miss the noise and confusion and splendor of this city. And I will miss my family—Papa, Tin-Tin, Gabi, Claire-Marie. And, yes, I will miss Maman. I love them, even when I do not like them very much. Even when I do not understand them at all.

Wednesday
18 July

WHEN I WENT to Grand-père's house today, Madelon told me there would be no more art lessons. She must have seen the disappointment in my face, because she added hurriedly, "Papa is worse. I cannot concentrate on anything else now."

There were purple smudges beneath her eyes and she appeared pale and listless.

When Maman came downstairs, she said that she must go home and see about supper. She asked Madelon to sit with Grand-père.

"I have an errand to run," Madelon replied. "Bodin can stay with him awhile."

A curious stillness came over Maman as she

searched Madelon's face. What errand, I wondered, was more important than staying with her dying father?

There was no time to ask Madelon if she had heard from John Mayfield.

Thursday 19 July

WHEN I WENT to see Claire-Marie this afternoon, she and Madelon were sitting in the courtyard. Claire-Marie was listening intently to something Madelon was saying, and they did not notice me until I was beside them. Claire-Marie was not happy to see me, but Madelon smiled and motioned for me to sit on the bench with her.

Soon after I arrived, Madelon said she must leave. Claire-Marie was obviously reluctant for her to go.

"Simone will keep you company," Madelon said. "I must get back to Papa."

"May I visit you later?" Claire-Marie asked.

"But of course," Madelon replied. "Whenever you like."

Claire-Marie has not been herself for some time, but today her mood was especially dark. My attempts at conversation were met with short, indifferent replies. It was only when I asked about Tante Vivienne that Claire-Marie came to life.

"Maman is recovering quite nicely," Claire-Marie said, "now that she knows Grand-père is leaving everything to her."

"Then she will not have to take in boarders," I said, puzzled that my cousin did not seem pleased by this.

"No, her life will change very little."

"And she will not have to sell Paulette and Eulalie," I added. And I will not have to help them escape, I thought, feeling relieved and strangely disappointed at the same time.

But before I had time to sort out my feelings, Claire-Marie said, "I have no interest in them. It is my *own* life I must think about now."

"I thought you knew what you wanted."

"Don't you understand anything, Simone?" Claire-Marie demanded. "Everything is different now. *Everything.*"

I asked what she meant, but my cousin clearly did not wish to continue our conversation.

Later, I asked Maman if Tante Vivienne still intends to sell Paulette and Eulalie.

"She will keep one of them," Maman said. "Probably Paulette, since she is older and more skilled."

"She would separate sisters who have been together all their lives?" I asked in astonishment.

"Simone, no more," Maman warned.

I must speak with Madelon. Paulette and Eulalie would not wish to be separated, and poor Eulalie is apparently still destined for the slave block. There seems to be no reason to alter our plans.

Friday
20 July

MADELON HAS HEARD from John Mayfield. She is to take the girls to him in four days' time.

I spoke with Paulette and Eulalie and told them that Tante Vivienne will be able to keep one of them. Their response was as I predicted—they will not be separated. And now that they have tasted the hope of freedom, they are willing to risk everything to leave New Orleans.

Grand-père has been in the deep sleep all day.

Saturday
21 July

I HAVE FINISHED packing everything I will take with me to Paris. I feel tremendous excitement, as well as sadness. I walk through these rooms that I have known all my life and wonder what it will feel like to wake each morning in a strange bed, to take my meals at a strange table.

While in this nostalgic mood, I did something that surprised me—no less than it surprised Maman. She was in the parlor, her head bent over her sewing. There was something so familiar and comforting in the way her delicate fingers worked the needle through the cloth, in the curve of her neck and the smooth sweep of her hair—and I thought, I may never see her this way again.

That was when I kissed Maman lightly on the cheek. Maman's head jerked up and her startled eyes met mine. Her expression was one of bafflement and uncertainty. But then she smiled, and that is the face I will take with me—the face that will remind me that my mother loves me.

Sunday
22 July

I HAVE BEEN such a fool! I trusted Madelon. I trusted Claire-Marie. I believed they cared for me as much as I cared for them. How very wrong I was!

After dinner, I tried to work on tomorrow's recitations, but I was too restless to concentrate. I could think of nothing except what lay ahead—the risks involved in helping Paulette and Eulalie leave the city. I am ashamed to say I also asked myself why I should take such risks, but I tried to banish those thoughts to the darkness where they belong. Finally, unable to stand this solitary dialogue with myself a moment longer, I left without telling anyone and walked to Grand-père's house. That is how I learned of Madelon and Claire-Marie's treachery.

I was surprised when Bodin said that Madelon was in her chamber with Claire-Marie. I had not expected to find my cousin there.

The door to Madelon's chamber was closed. I knocked and Madelon called out for me to enter.

When I opened the door, the first thing I saw was Madelon's huge trunk in the center of the room. It was open, and filled with her beautiful gowns. The bed was covered with bonnets and slippers. Claire-Marie was filling a valise with Madelon's undergarments.

I knew at once what they were doing. And had I not grasped this on my own, the discomfort in their expressions when they saw me would have given them away.

"You are leaving," I said stupidly to Madelon. Of course she was leaving! Why else would she be packing? Then my eyes fell on two bulging valises in the corner. They belonged to Tante Vivienne. "And Claire-Marie is going with you."

Claire-Marie took a step toward me. The sympathy in her eyes was nearly more than I could bear.

"You were leaving without telling me," I accused her.

"I was going to tell you," she said softly. "After we

finished packing, I intended to go to your house."

"Of course we were going to tell you," Madelon said.

"But *I* was supposed to go with you!"

"I never imagined you were serious," Madelon replied. "I assumed your talk of Paris was only a child's fancy."

"I am not a child! And I told you I was going with you."

"Your mother would never permit it," Madelon said with a hint of impatience in her voice.

I turned to Claire-Marie. "And your mother will?" I asked.

A look of defiance flashed across my cousin's face. "I am leaving a letter for her to find after we are gone."

"Please understand, *chérie,*" Madelon said gently. She reached out to stroke my hair, but I pulled away.

"I understand perfectly." I was trying not to cry, but my aunt's face blurred and I was forced to wipe away tears.

"No, you do not," Madelon said wearily. "Come, sit beside me and I will explain so that you *can* understand."

I allowed myself to be led to the bed, but I fastened my eyes on the floral carpet and refused to look at her.

What Madelon told me is this: There is no grand

house in Paris; she had to sell it to pay off debts when her husband died. She is very nearly penniless, so she came back to New Orleans to convince Grand-père to leave his estate to her. Just as Claire-Marie suspected all along. And yet, Claire-Marie is going away with her!

"I know this sounds horrible to you," Madelon said, "but you have no idea how frightening it is to be on your own with no money. You have a mother and father who give you everything. Tell me, Simone, have you ever wanted for anything?"

I looked from my aunt to Claire-Marie. "You have never wanted for anything, either," I said to my cousin. "You will break Tante Vivienne's heart if you leave."

"All Maman has ever cared about is her own comfort," Claire-Marie replied, looking angry, yet close to tears. "I thought she loved Papa. I thought her grief was for him. But now that her financial future is settled, she no longer weeps for my father—nor will she weep for me."

How heartless she has become! "That is not true," I said.

"I know what is true," she said harshly. "Maman needed the promise of my sons. That is the only reason Grand-père is leaving his estate to her—so that the house and the Agneau name can be passed on to them.

Now that she has everything, I am no longer useful to her."

"In Paris, Claire-Marie will have her choice of young men to marry," Madelon said. "She will not have to fulfill anyone's dreams but her own."

"And what will you do?" I demanded of my aunt.

Madelon shrugged. "I am not as young and beautiful as I once was, but there are still men who find me attractive. I will choose one who can give me what I need and I will marry him."

I turned away before they could read the feelings in my face.

"I know you are angry," Madelon said. She sounded weary.

"Angry?" I spun around, ready to spit out every accusation I could think of. But something stopped me. The look of exhaustion on her face, perhaps. Or the realization that I was feeling much more than anger toward her.

Madelon's eyes searched mine, and she said softly, "I never meant to hurt you, Simone."

A sharp ache gnawed at my heart. If she had held her arms out to me then, I would have run into them. But she only looked at me, unable or unwilling to offer any more comfort.

"When are you leaving?" I asked stiffly.

"Our ship sails early in the morning."

"And what of Paulette and Eulalie? You were to take them to John Mayfield in two days' time."

"What does she mean?" Claire-Marie asked Madelon.

"So you have no intention of helping them?" I demanded of my aunt before she could respond to Claire-Marie.

"You can take them just as well," Madelon said.

"But everything you said about slavery being wrong," I protested. "About Paulette and Eulalie being no different from you and me—"

"Yes, slavery is wrong," Madelon said with a frown, "but I cannot change the world. And right now I must think about myself."

I had the strangest feeling that I was seeing and hearing the real Madelon for the first time. But it seemed unreal to me. I still could not believe I had been so wrong about her.

Claire-Marie was clasping my arm and saying, "Simone, listen to me. Simone!"

I tore my eyes from Madelon's face to look at my cousin.

"Promise that you will say nothing to Maman and Tante Delphine until after the ship has sailed," Claire-Marie pleaded. "Promise me, Simone."

I promised. But while I said the words, I was thinking about the promise Madelon had made to Paulette and Eulalie. And how casually she had broken that promise when it did not suit her plans.

"When is John Mayfield expecting the girls?" I asked.

"Tuesday night at ten o'clock," Madelon said as she placed another gown into the trunk.

"It was exciting to think of helping slaves escape in the dead of night, wasn't it, Madelon?" I asked. "You never cared about Paulette and Eulalie. It was taking the risk and feeling important that appealed to you."

She did not answer me, and I left the room without saying good-bye to either of them. Walking home, I remembered Maman's concern that I would emulate Madelon. She had *known* what Madelon was like. It was not as I thought, that she envied our closeness. She had wanted to protect me. Another startling realization to add to the many this day!

Monday
23 July

I AWOKE EARLY this morning to the sounds of Azura preparing breakfast. It was all so ordinary—the banging of pots, the cooing of pigeons on the roof, the smell of strong coffee wafting up the stairs—that for a moment I felt drowsily blissful and safe. Then I remembered that Madelon and Claire-Marie were leaving this morning. In fact, their ship had probably already sailed.

Despair settled over me and I thought I might weep, which made me think of Grand-père Jules's words to Madelon: *Tears are weak!* He is not a person to admire and respect—this man who can suffocate babies without apparent conscience—but he has survived a difficult life. And through it all, he has refused to give in to despair. At least *that* is an admirable quality.

I lay in bed thinking about my grandfather. Grand-père is a man of great strength and determination. He could have put that strength to good use; but instead he has used it to bully everyone in his life into submission. I despise that about him, but I cannot despise *him*. He is my grandfather. The bonds of blood and history are there, whether I wish to acknowledge them or not. But I can make different choices than he has. I can use the Agneau strength to become whomever I wish to be.

After a while, I no longer felt like crying. I am deeply hurt that Claire-Marie could think of leaving without telling me, that our years together apparently mean so little to her. I am grieved that Madelon could betray me, as well as Maman, Tante Vivienne, Paulette, and Eulalie. But Claire-Marie and Madelon were also free to choose, and I can do nothing about their choices.

I hear Tante Vivienne's voice downstairs. It is too early for visiting. I know why she has come.

Later

MAMAN GAVE TANTE Vivienne a cup of ginseng tea to calm her and sent Tin-Tin to the docks to see if the ship had sailed. It had. When Tante Vivienne learned that Claire-Marie was truly on her way to France, my aunt dissolved into tears once more.

Maman has questioned me at length. At first, she was not satisfied with my insistence that Madelon and Claire-Marie did not confide in me. But they never planned to share their secret with me, and the pain this causes is so apparent, Maman has ceased to badger me.

While Maman was occupied with consoling Tante Vivienne, I went to see Véronique. She was sweeping the walk in the courtyard.

"You knew they were leaving," I said to her.

She nodded and continued to sweep.

"Does Grand-père know?"

"Monsieur Jules asked for Madelon, and Bodin was forced to tell him."

"Is he distressed?"

Véronique ceased her sweeping and glanced up at the window of Grand-père's chamber. "He refuses medicine and food," she said. "I believe he is ready to die."

I was not prepared for the pity that filled my heart when I heard this. I thought of my grandfather lying alone and weak in his great bed, deserted by the daughter and granddaughter he loved most—perhaps the only two people he loved at all. What was it all for, Grandpère? I asked silently. What had the years of scheming and cruelty come to but a lonely death in a darkened chamber?

"I will go see him," I said.

Véronique did not look surprised that I would voluntarily seek out my grandfather's company.

"When the time comes for you and Bodin to leave New Orleans, I know someone who will help you," I added.

Again, Véronique's face betrayed no surprise. She just nodded and said, "Bring Paulette and Eulalie here tomorrow night. I will have clothing packed for them."

"You know about their escape!"

A smile touched Véronique's lips. "Monsieur Jules is not the only one who knows what happens in this house."

"Help me understand, Véronique." Pain coursed through my heart once more. "How could she make them such an important promise and then walk away?"

Véronique shook her head. "I cannot see into another's soul. Missy Madelon was a selfish child and she grew to be a selfish woman. Perhaps because she had no one to teach her to be otherwise, or because she lost so much so early. Who is to say why she feels she must grab everything for herself? Now," Véronique said gently, "go see Monsieur Jules and make your peace."

Grand-père was awake when I entered his chamber. His eyes followed me as I approached the bed.

"*Bonjour,* Grand-père," I said.

The black eyes bored into me, but he said nothing.

"How are you feeling?"

Again, no response.

The cat walked across the bed and rubbed against me. I stroked him as I studied Grand-père's face: the sharp thrust of his cheekbones, the narrow nose, the curved lips. Maman and her sisters had inherited his features, but the glowering expression was his alone.

"Do you not know better than to stare like an idiot child?" he demanded suddenly. His voice was weak, but it still resonated with authority.

I sat down beside the bed, never taking my eyes from his. It was as though we were playing a game to see who would look away first, and each of us was determined to win.

"Have you been taught none of the social graces?" he asked coldly. "Has your mother taught you nothing about how to conduct yourself?"

"My mother has taught me to conduct myself as an Agneau," I replied, my voice as cold as his. "I *am* an Agneau, every bit as much as Claire-Marie."

His brows drew together in a deeper scowl.

"You are not an easy man to love, Grand-père," I said, "not an easy man to love at all."

And he blinked! Only the tiniest flutter of eyelid and lash, but enough to show me that my words had startled him.

I reached for the book on his bedside table and opened it to the page where Maman had placed her embroidered bookmark. The cat settled into my lap.

I was surprised to see that Maman had been reading to Grand-père from a well-worn book of French children's stories. It occurred to me that perhaps this was a book *ma mère* had loved as a child. Could it be that Grand-père had read these same stories to *her* long ago?

"I will read to you until Véronique comes with your medicine," I said.

His scowl was formidable then, but he did not voice an objection.

I began to read. After a time, I stole a glance at him. His black eyes were still on me, but the ferocious gleam in them had dimmed. I continued to read, and when my hand found his on top of the counterpane, he did not pull away.

Late night

I CANNOT SLEEP. As hard as I try to shut down my mind, it will not be stilled. I picture Claire-Marie on the deck of a sailing ship, her silky hair whipped by the wind, her face flushed with anticipation. Perhaps she misses me, as I miss her, but I cannot visualize her as anything but happy and excited as she begins her great adventure. I picture Madelon beside her, pleased and amused by Claire-Marie's joy. I doubt that Madelon thinks of me at all.

Tuesday 24 July

THE DAY IS hot and clear. We will have a bright moon to travel by tonight. I will wear Tin-Tin's boots. And I will take this journal with me in case they find me gone and search my chamber. Maman is more likely to forgive me for helping slaves escape than for describing her as I have in these pages.

I sit in the courtyard with my sketchbook open but

untouched. I have been thinking how Grand-père's dreams for his family have shaped each of us, me no less than Madelon and Claire-Marie. I suspect that long after Grand-père Jules is gone, my aunt and cousin will live in the shadow of those dreams. But *I* will not!

Evening

PAULETTE AND EULALIE were waiting for me in Tante Vivienne's courtyard. We made it here to Grand-père's house without incident. The girls are changing into sturdy shoes while Véronique packs a change of clothing for them.

Paulette and Eulalie are surprisingly calm. I am trying to be.

I told Maman that I was weary, then retired shortly after supper. Fortunately, Tante Vivienne is still with us, and her needs occupy Maman's time and concentration. I left by the kitchen door and do not think I was observed. With luck, I will be safely in my bed before anyone misses me.

This afternoon I had the strongest urge to tell Tin-Tin what I was doing and to ask him to come with us. But it would have been unfair to involve him. He might have come simply because he feared for my safety.

I hear Véronique and the girls coming down the

stairs. It is time to leave. I will tuck this journal into the drawer of Grand-père's desk. If I return, it will be waiting for me. And if I do not return, it will no longer matter if my family reads the words in these pages.

Wednesday morning
25 July

TWO PIECES OF news: One, Paulette and Eulalie have left the city. Two, I am confined to my chamber once again. According to Tin-Tin, Maman plans to keep me imprisoned here until I leave to marry.

Last night's journey through the swamp was more terrifying than anything I could have imagined. Had I known how difficult it would be, I doubt I would have found the courage to attempt it. But luckily for Paulette and Eulalie, we began the long journey in ignorance. It was their hope that sustained me when my naïveté began to crumble in that great black swamp that seemed eager to devour us.

I will record the events of our experience here, and if I am ever so rash as to consider such an action again, perhaps rereading these words will dissuade me. But triumph has a way of dissolving even the sharpest memories of fear. As now, only hours after the ordeal, I sit in my soft bed with sunlight pouring through the open shutters and I think, We could have died in that swamp, but oh, what a glorious adventure it was! And more importantly, I think of the joy on Paulette's and Eulalie's faces when the journey was done, and I know that I would do it all again.

It was dark when we left Grand-père's house. The few people we met seemed to pay us no mind; but still, my heart thumped frantically for fear that we would be questioned and would fail to give a believable response. It was not until we left the city behind that I began to breathe more easily.

The night was clear and bright, with a moon that was nearly full. This was fortunate, because we could see the road ahead, and I would be able to recognize the spot where we would leave it and proceed through the swamp to the Bernadins' summer house. But a bright moon could also mean disaster if we were to come upon a patrol, for they would surely see us and ask what we were doing outside the city at night.

For the longest time, the only sounds I heard were frogs croaking in the swamp and the swish of my skirts. Then Eulalie began to hum a tune nervously under her breath.

"Hush!" Paulette hissed at her. "Do you want someone to hear you?"

"I'm sorry," Eulalie whispered.

We continued on in silence.

At last, we came to the place where trees thinned out alongside the road and we could see moonlight sparkling silver on a pool of black water.

I stopped. "This is where we leave the road," I said softly. "There is a trail of solid ground through the swamp."

"The swamp?" Eulalie echoed. "I never go into the swamp."

"Do you know your way?" Paulette asked me, sounding uncertain.

"I have walked this path dozens of times," I replied. In fact, I had been on the trail only once with Lucien, and that had been in broad daylight.

"Come on," Paulette said to her sister, and reached for Eulalie's hand.

They followed me off the road and onto a path that circled the water and then disappeared into darkness. The earth felt spongy beneath my feet. As I walked, I tried to clear my mind of thoughts that came unbidden and threatened to shake my confidence: of snakes twisted around tree limbs, ready to drop on unsuspecting prey; of alligators emerging lazily from the water and stretching their great lengths across the trail; of wild hogs and every other sort of vicious animal that would view the three of us as a welcome supper indeed.

As we moved deeper into the swamp, less and less moonlight penetrated the dense growth of trees and vines, until finally we could see nothing. I had not even thought to bring a candle, and I silently cursed my lack of foresight. Unsure how to proceed, I came to an abrupt stop. Paulette and Eulalie, who had been following close behind, stumbled into me.

"Can you see anything?" Paulette asked.

"No," I admitted, "but the ground is firm, so we are still on the path. We will walk slowly and feel our way."

"It is so dark," Eulalie said in a small voice. "We could be lost and no one would ever find us."

"Nonsense," I snapped, irritated because she had given voice to my own worst thoughts. "This trail leads to the house. We just have to follow it."

We set out again. And I thought, How amazing that they will put aside their fears and follow me into the bowels of the swamp—based on nothing more than a slender thread of faith that I know what I am doing! That was the most frightening part of all, their faith in me. It was humbling, beyond anything else I had ever experienced. That was the only time during our long night together that I thought I might burst into tears.

Why am I doing this? I asked myself. I wondered if, like Madelon, I was only trying to feel important by helping the girls escape. Perhaps that was part of it. I know it wasn't the excitement that prompted me—because the terror I felt left no room for excitement.

I finally came to this conclusion: I was helping Paulette and Eulalie because I do not believe that any-one can own another person. It was Madelon who showed me this. It was she who made me see Paulette and Eulalie as people instead of property. If Madelon had not come back to New Orleans, I would not have gone to the St. Louis Hotel and seen the girl on the slave block. I might never have questioned the morality of slav-ery. When I realized this, any anger I felt toward my aunt disappeared.

It was more than art Madelon taught me, after all.

As the night wore on, I tried not to think about the horrors that lurked all around us. Instead, I focused on keeping to the path—and on the girls' belief in me. There was no way I could turn back now. And no way I could fail. Paulette and Eulalie had handed me their lives, and I could do nothing less than see them safely to the man who would give them a chance for freedom.

We inched along in the darkness. Even so, Paulette stumbled and fell, pulling me down with her. She groaned as we landed on the wet ground.

Eulalie squatted beside us. "Are you hurt?" she asked her sister anxiously.

"My ankle."

I found Paulette's foot and probed. Her ankle was already beginning to swell.

"I think it is only a sprain," I said. "Let me loosen the laces on your shoe."

"How can you walk?" Eulalie asked. "We will have to stay here. We never should have come."

"I can walk," Paulette said, and began to struggle to her feet.

"Not yet," I cautioned. "Rest awhile."

But Paulette was already standing. She could not walk, however, without assistance. The path was not wide enough for three, so Paulette leaned on me and Eulalie followed behind.

Our progress slowed to a crawl. Paulette tried to muffle her whimpers of pain but did not always succeed. Eulalie lost their bundle of clothing in the deep water and we could not retrieve it. I was covered with muck from head to toe, the mosquitoes swarmed and stung relentlessly, and my arm throbbed from bearing Paulette's weight.

Through those terrible, endless hours, when it seemed that we would never make it into the light again, all manner of images flashed through my mind. I saw Claire-Marie and Madelon, both laughing and beautiful, and felt no resentment toward them. What I felt was the purest love I had ever known. I saw Tin-Tin, so serious and worried about me, and Gabi working on a block of pale marble. I saw Papa, his eyes tender when he looked at me. And I saw Maman, her arms stretched out to pull me close. Perhaps exhaustion and fear had muddled my thinking, but it seemed that they were all there with me, and they were saying, We will be here to see you through.

Paulette's voice brought me back to the moment. "Is that a light?" she asked softly.

And it was. A faint glow hardly bigger than a firefly pierced the darkness ahead.

We stumbled toward it, until at last I could see a window filled with lantern light.

A dog barked at our approach. The door of the house opened, and a man came out to the porch.

"Madelon?" he called softly, speaking her name with an American accent.

"I came in Madelon's place," I answered.

We made our way into the clearing, and the man started toward us. "The girls are safe?" he asked.

"Quite safe," I replied, and Eulalie began to weep.

Wednesday noon

I MUST RECORD with sadness that Grand-père Jules died last night. Before going home, I stopped to tell Véronique that the girls had made it to John Mayfield's house. Grand-père had already slipped away in his sleep. I went to his chamber and stood beside the bed. What he would have said could he have seen me then, filthy and wet, my face red and swollen from mosquito bites!

I looked into Grand-père's face and he seemed to be asleep. A restful sleep, without torment or bitterness. The cat lay beside him, watching me.

"Your master is finally at peace," I said.

I had only a moment to bid my grandfather farewell before I heard Maman's and Papa's voices in the corridor. I left Grand-père's chamber and went to meet them.

Wednesday evening

AZURA MADE A paste for the mosquito bites. It caused me some concern when she began to dab the stuff on my face and arms, but her touch was gentle and the medicine has eased the discomfort. If it was magic Mambo Azura used, then it was good magic.

Papa is more perplexed with me than angry—although he is not pleased to be paying Tante Vivienne for Paulette and Eulalie after all. Maman is angry enough for both of them. Tin-Tin says when Maman realized I was gone, she was worried. She had no idea where I might have gone or why. It was Véronique who told her where I was, and that is when *ma mère*'s worry turned to anger. But last night, when I left Grand-père's chamber and came face-to-face with her, Maman took one look at my bedraggled self and then embraced me—wet and dirty though I was. It was just as I had imagined in the swamp.

"How could you do this?" Maman asked. She gave me a little shake, but still she held me. "You could have died in that swamp," she said, and her arms tightened around me.

But just as I relaxed against her, so relieved to be home and held close in those arms, she pulled away and glared at me. "I am surprised," she said, "that you did not spirit Azura away, as well, while you were about it."

"Delphine, look at her...," Papa began, obviously distressed by my appearance. "What she has been through."

"What she has put *herself* through," Maman corrected him. "Go home at once," she said to me. "I cannot think about this now—I must see to Papa. Clean yourself up and stay in your chamber until I return."

I will be on my knees to the Blessed Mother, contemplating my sins for a very long time. Maman will have me embroidering pillow slips until my fingers bleed. She will teach me responsibility and duty if it is the last thing she does.

While I write, Grand-père's cat dozes in a spot of sun at the foot of my bed. He appears to have decided to stay.

Maman does not yet know about the cat. She will be displeased. But after she has lectured me and complained to Papa, she will say, "Since you have taken it upon yourself to bring this useless creature into the house, Simone, it is your duty to care for it."

Then she will send me to the kitchen to pour a bowl of milk for the cat.

I know this because Maman never changes. And that is her way.

Afterword

Following the Civil War, articulate political leaders emerged from the *gens de couleur libre*. But their voices, and their hopes for social equality, were drowned in a flood of racism. Many white Americans responded with bitterness to the abolishment of slavery and directed their hostility toward all people of color. As a result, the *gens de couleur libre* lost many of the freedoms and privileges they had enjoyed before the war. They could do nothing to arrest the growing prejudice they faced, nor the restrictive legislation born of that prejudice.

What became of the eighteen thousand *gens de couleur libre* who lived in New Orleans before the Civil War? Some moved north and hid their African heritage. Others migrated to California and Mexico, claiming Hispanic ancestry. But most remained in Louisiana, where they witnessed the death of a culture that was unlike any other this country has known.

In the *Journal of Negro History* 2 (1917), African-American historian Alice Dunbar-Nelson said of the *gens de couleur libre:*

> *There is no State in the Union, hardly any spot of like size on the globe, where the man of color has lived so intensely, made so much progress, been of such historical importance and yet about whom so comparatively little is known. His history is like the Mardi Gras of the city of New Orleans, beautiful and mysterious and wonderful, but with a serious thought underlying it all. May it be better known to the world some day.*